Come and get it...

Dinnertime came. I was faint with hunger. The table looked great, heaped with stacks of tortillas and all the trimmings. Finally Dad dipped his ladle in the pot and brought up . . . that thing. It was a long thick braid of human hair. Mom gagged. Even soaked with chili you could see it had been blondish-brown, a kid's hair. Heck. We'd seen enough photographs in that house to recognize the kid with blondish-brown braids. It was so gross that Dad carried the whole thing straight out to the trash, pot and all. . . .

Our appetites destroyed, we had a whole lot of time to ask ourselves who had been able to get in and put it there, and why. . . .

Other Point paperbacks
you will enjoy:

The Cat-Dogs and Other Tales of Horror
edited by Anne Finnis

In Camera and Other Stories
by Robert Westall

The Leaving and Other Stories
by Budge Wilson

Thirteen
edited by T. Pines

PLEASE DO NOT TOUCH

A Collection of Stories

JUDITH GOROG

SCHOLASTIC INC.
New York Toronto London Auckland Sydney

ISBN 0-590-46683-6

12 11 10 9 8 7 6 5 4 3 2 1   9   5 6 7 8 9/9 0/0

Printed in the U.S.A.   01

For the van Raalte clan,
John and Andreé, Kirsten and James,
Oma and Opa, and the ones born to
and married to:
livers and lovers and storytellers, every one.

Contents

PLEASE DO NOT TOUCH

IN
THE
GALLERY

There are two ways to visit *The Gallery Pitu*. For the timid, the housebound, or the lazy, there is interactive television. Yes, it is clumsy, but from the comfort and safety of your couch, you can send the eye of a television camera into the gallery, from one exhibit to another and, if you are skilled enough, you can enter an exhibit. Like the artist who made these works, you can snoop, poke into other people's closets. You can eavesdrop.

Of course, the television eye does not see as yours does, does not note movement far off to the side. The eye of the camera does not offer those colors more felt than seen, nor can it pick up the smells, the feel of things. Furthermore, the controls for directing the camera eye are so awkward to use. You can easily find your snooping eye stuck in the closet, blinded by a blue wool sweater, when the announcement of closing time comes at The Gallery Pitu.

You have the time and the courage; you can travel to the city, to the ancient part of the town, where the streets are narrow, more curved than straight. You can walk along sidewalks lined with slender trees, each one encircled by a small wrought-iron fence. You can turn a corner to discover a tiny park jutting out where two streets meet in a Y. The park has grass, tall trees, benches on which old ladies sit in coats and hats of shades of lavender, their heads bent over their books, reading. Inside the park you hear the sounds of leaves rustling, of water flowing in the fountain, of birds and squirrels, with the roar of city traffic muted, as if it were far away.

There is one large swing, which creaks pleasantly as you use it. Two gentlemen in tweed jackets, knitted ties, and soft fedoras, each with a cane at his side, play checkers at a stone table. At a second table, a boy and girl are playing chess. No, don't linger. They don't want your advice. Just opposite the park, at a place where the sun still reaches into the narrow street, you can see it — The Gallery Pitu. There is a sign, with the name painted once in fresh gilt on wood; but you can still see faded black characters, traces of words not always in languages you recognize, as if the sign has been painted many times. Ironwork decorates the front of the *building and the door. There is a largish plate-glass window. When you look inside, you see the lens of a TV camera, a pile of beat-up skateboards, shadows moving, but no people. The door is locked, as so many are in cities these days. You ring the bell. A buzzer responds. The door opens, closes behind you. The walls are gray, the floor dark-stained wood, the ceiling white tin, beaten into elaborate designs. The smell is empty.*

There is no catalog. The artist never permits one. This artist (some say it is a woman) makes each work as a record of her snooping. She peeps and peers, follows and listens, spies and keeps records. You can follow where she has been: into a house or a room, into yesterday, today, or tomorrow.

You decide: You will first look at the whole exhibit, stroll past each and every one of the works, before you choose one to follow. Touching is permitted in The Gallery Pitu. Touching takes you there.

You try hard to stick to the center of the aisle. Right and left are doors and windows; a staircase leads up from a place on your left. Down there, a mirror, something passing. You turn your head. On the wall, a scrap of yellow newspaper. The date is eighteen-something, torn, but an ad for a magic show. Beside it is a half-eaten cookie, a laundry stub with strange symbols, and that thing. You know what it is: curved heavy-wire hoops at one end; at the other, a wooden handle smooth with wear. You know that's a rug beater, from the olden days. The artist has given this one a name. You lean closer to read it, but the print is so small. You know you have not touched anything, not even the wall, but still you feel yourself falling forward, feel the wall closing around you. You find yourself on a staircase, listening to a boy ahead of you. He's muttering. . . .

Jemmy's
Halloween

Fake. That magician was a fake. Last night everybody in town saw it. Now he's gone. Skipped out. Didn't even leave the money for room and board.

Jemmy watches as his mother unlocks the door to the room she had rented to the chap with the oily black hair, the one who called himself the Great Mafisti. Gone. Gone. He'd managed to take his clothes, but left behind that magician stuff: a tall black hat, black cape lined with frayed satin, a walking stick (the tip is no more real silver than the knob on the bedpost). There's a pair of poorly mended white gloves in need of a wash, and the sheet he used for his fake disappearing act. Well, *he* sure disappeared, even though he couldn't make anything else disappear from under that old gray sheet.

Jemmy's mother strips the bed, takes down the curtains. Jemmy rolls up the rug, takes it downstairs, and slings it over the line. Beating the rug will help. Jemmy is so mad. That fake "Great" was one solid disappointment. He was crabby, greedy at meals, and then went and gave the town a miserable failure of a show, and for his encore, skipped out without paying. Jemmy and his mother have little enough, and boarders who leave without paying, after eating them out of house and home, well. . . . It will hurt in the weeks to come. Jemmy had seen his mother eyeing the stuff left behind. That fellow's tattered bag won't bring much. The hat and cape? Who'd buy them? Jemmy shrugs, starts beating the rug, doing as his mother had said: "Beat every speck of that fellow's dust out of my rug!"

After a time, Jemmy turns the rug over, beats some more, forcing himself to hit it hard, thinking that every whack will build up his muscles, right arm, left arm.

As Jemmy gets tired, he hits more slowly, but his thoughts go faster and faster. Jemmy is turning over a different problem, the one he's been thinking about for weeks. Every other kid in town has been furiously at work, always in secret. Jem doesn't even know what his best friend is planning to wear for Halloween. Jemmy has let things slide too long.

"Too long." Jemmy can hear his mother call, her voice full of impatience. "Don't beat that rug to death. Come inside. Wash down the room while I get this laundry done."

Jem washes the room while his mother stirs the boiling sheets. By the time he finishes, she is ready for him to help her put the heavy wet wash through the wringer, through the rinses, and get the sheets out onto the line. "But first, go bring in that rug. And don't shake it. We don't want dust all over the laundry."

"Yes'mmm."

One after the other, the sheets go up onto the lines, where they snap and crack in the strong prairie wind. Jem's mother tugs at the magician's vanishing sheet, testing the quality. It has come out nice and white, except for a funny mark in black ink on the hem of one corner.

"Mommm?" Jemmy has to get her help. "Momm, what can I be for Halloween?"

She frowns. "You could use his cape and hat, and his stick?"

"Come on! Everybody would laugh at me."

"That's the point. You could do it for a joke," she suggests.

"Don't you have any better ideas?"

"You could be a ghost."

Jemmy groans. "I've been a ghost. Nobody would be fooled. I gotta do something different."

Jemmy's mother does not have a single good

idea that day, nor the day afterward, nor the day after that.

Jemmy can't ask his friends. They are all so smug and smiling about their costumes, sure they will fool everybody. And Halloween is even bigger than usual this year. Everybody is talking; everybody is saying that *everybody* is gonna be SOMEthing. And what about ol' Mrs. Peabody, who lives in the biggest, fanciest house in town? Mrs. Peabody — who has all sorts of amazing things in her house, including a glass case that holds a real mummy brought right there into her house all the way from Egypt; people are saying that she is going to dress up in layers and layers of cloth pantaloons, with scarves and all. And a velvet vest all covered with sequins. She is going to be a Hareem Lady, they say. The talk and excitement get to be so much that even Jemmy's mother suddenly announces that she thinks she might wear a costume.

Jemmy does not like his mother's idea one bit. How can she be thinking of her own costume when all she has offered Jem is some sheet to be a ghost. When Jemmy says angrily that he will not be a ghost, his mother says, "Well, then, I might just be a ghost myself and scare the daylights out of everyone who comes a trick or treating."

Discouraged and mad, Jemmy cannot stop thinking about going to trick or treat at Mrs.

Peabody's, as he has done every year of his life. He *has* to have a good costume, so he can go there and see all the other costumes, see Mrs. Peabody and her friends all dressed up. Most years, Mrs. Peabody calls all the children into the parlor to explain their costumes, to sing or dance, or to tell a funny story. You get cider passed by the butler, and cookies passed by the maid, and something good to take home with you. Jemmy has to be there. He can just see Mrs. Peabody's front parlor right now in his mind.

And that's it! Seeing the room gives Jem the idea he needs. Without telling his mother, Jemmy slips the magician's sheet out of the linen closet, where his mother had put it with the other sheets after she finished ironing it smooth and flat. His mother can use any old sheet for her old ghost costume. That fake magician owes Jem *this* sheet. After all, how many times did Jemmy black that man's boots, and never got a penny for it?

Jemmy takes the sheet, and on Halloween he goes to his best friend's house. For this costume, Jem needs some help. At Buck's house, Jem cuts the sheet into long strips. Then, one after another, Buck winds those strips around Jem's body until Jem is the finest, most mysterious mummy in the whole world. At the very end of the winding, Buck tucks the part of the sheet with the black writing into a place on the back of Jem's neck, where the ink won't show.

Jem can see and walk, all stiff-legged, and he can drink cider and eat cookies, carefully, because Buck has left open slits for Jem's eyes and for his mouth.

After dark, Buck leads Jem through the swirling crowds of costumes, from house to house, and what a success they are! Nobody, not even Jem's own mother, guesses who Jem is. House to house they go, street to street, and to the parlor of Mrs. Peabody's, where Jem makes mysterious Egyptian mummy sounds for his part of the show. It is the greatest Halloween ever.

Late that night, back at Buck's house, Jem stands still while Buck starts unwinding the strips of magician's sheet. Buck unwinds and unwinds, and Jem waits and waits, listening to Buck's breathing, which sounds peculiar.

"Jem?" Buck whispers.

"Ullfppp," Jem replies in mysterious Egyptian noises.

"That magician wasn't a fake after all."

"Eleep?"

"Look."

"Urrpp?"

"You *see* yourself, where I've taken the wraps off? You better say something, 'cause I can't see you. Here's all this sheet tore in strips, lying in a pile on the floor. And no sign of you."

Jem walks over to the looking glass and peers

into it. There, reflected in the surface of the mirror, Jem can see his two eyes, his lips, faintly there. But of the rest of his body, there is not a trace.

In the mirror, those eyes stare, those lips part, as Jem answers Buck, in mysterious Egyptian mummy sounds.

You want to help. Your own mouth opens to offer a suggestion, but, before you can make a sound, you find yourself slipping backward away from them, as if you were nothing more than a television camera eye. You travel in this way for what seems a long time, with no sounds, no smells, just movement. At last, you reach a forest. You can smell and hear the leaves soughing, and more, someone talking to you, a woman who takes your hand and leads you to a place where you can see.

Hillside House

That house, which never deserved to be known as a killer, was built to stand all alone in the woods on the side of the hill, at a point where the opposite hillside fell away to offer the house a magnificent view of the hills and valleys below. There, in the heavy woods, the house was protected from the harsh winds that occasionally buffeted the ridge above it, while the leaves of every tree around it swayed gently in the breezes that moved down the hillside. From every window, the occupants could see hills, forest, sky, meadows, in velvet patterns across the valleys below.

Built more than one hundred years ago, the house was sound and solid. Its brick fireplaces were set with tiles that stirred the imaginations of one generation of children after another. The huge living room was lined entirely with wood. The ceiling in between the heavy beams, the bookcases, the walls and floor were of a combination of woods that gave the rooms a beauty both satisfying to the eye and comforting to the heart no matter what sort of storm raged through the hills. Because it had been enlarged and changed over the years, the house had plenty of small, cozy spots, and a dining room big enough for a real Thanksgiving feast.

For the house, everything changed when the highway came. At first, the family that lived in the house fought the plan for the road, but in vain. The highway ate up part of the hillside above the house. The concrete arches of the highway shadowed the house. The roar of passing trucks, the honking of horns, the screech of brakes or of tires skidding on pavement, the occasional crunch of metal upon metal, metal against concrete, and even upon flesh, the shriek of sirens, the sounds of dying; these noises filled the house.

The family abandoned the house.

Robin and Tom, newly engaged to be married, discovered the empty house on the hillside, deep in the shadows of the great highway, one bright Saturday while they were out bicycling over the back roads of the hills. Actually, the house was a discovery for Robin. Tom had grown up around those hills, and his uncle, with whom they were visiting, was the one who said to them, *"You don't want that house."*

But Robin did want it, highway or not, and Robin all her life had always got what she wanted. Buying it was easy. Standing where it did, under that highway, it was a bargain. Getting the house in shape was not much more difficult. It had been well constructed and well cared for all those years, and had stood empty for . . . how long? Oh, a few years at the worst.

Uncle Ned knew, but he said only, *"You don't want that house."*

Robin and Tom got married, went away for a brief honeymoon, and returned to live in the house. At three in the afternoon, they carried their bags inside. Tom put on his favorite music. They unpacked, had a coffee on the terrace while they watched the change of light on the hills and in the valleys below the house. They did hear the noise of traffic from the highway, but were able to ignore it.

By nightfall, however, no amount of ignoring, no music could keep the sounds from their ears. The house was filled with the vibrations of the roadway; full of the roar, the shriek, the skidding tires, the silence, followed by the thud, as rushing machine struck . . . what?

The presence of the highway filled the house, shook the pictures from the walls, made the furniture dance in the rooms. Robin, her eyes white with terror, hands covering her ears, could not keep the sounds away, could not sleep, cried out that she would run up to the roadway and rip it from the hillside, but the roar of the highway increased, and a violent crash swallowed the sound of Robin's last scream.

Tom, avoiding his uncle, abandoned the house, moved far away, and tried to forget. Uncle Ned shook his head and muttered, "Told her she didn't want that house."

The house stood empty for years, until Beatrice, who had made millions in real estate, saw it and agreed that no one would want it . . . where it stood.

Uncle Ned grumbled, "*You don't want that house.*"

Nevertheless, moving houses was his business, so Uncle Ned moved the house to a hillside far, far from that highway, far from any highway.

Once again, the house stood in a setting that befitted it, and sure enough, buyers came from right and left. In no time, Beatrice had sold the house and made a handsome profit. Uncle Ned, who had been called in to consult about some repairs, met the new owners. When he told them, "*You don't want that house,*" they thought he was a rustic eccentric.

Those new owners — their names have been lost to us — lasted in the house one half of one night. They were far from any road, and yet they were disturbed beyond measure, awakened by the sound and feel of heavy traffic as if a great highway ran right above the house. The thud of vehicle on flesh, the cries of the dying, and the echoing shrieks of Robin's terror were too much for the new owners.

Uncle Ned shook his head at the news. "Told them they didn't want that house."

Years passed. The house stood shut up on the hillside. Beatrice died; Uncle Ned died. Stories about the house died.

By the time we bought the house, it needed quite a bit of repair. The window sashes, the frames, all were needing to be replaced. Many panes of glass lay shattered amid leaves and forest debris on the floors. A rather sizeable colony of bats occupied the attic. Mice had nested in every cupboard. Still, the basic wood and stone of the house were sound. The house could be repaired. Slowly, we set to work. We built homes for the bats, and once we had begun to scrape and pound and paint and clean in the house, they moved to their new quarters with apparent satisfaction. It took us years to make the repairs, for we lacked both money and time. While we worked, doors and windows stood open, the breezes of the hillside passing freely through. Our coming and going was random, whenever we could manage a few hours or perhaps a full day of work. It was odd that whenever we came, we had a visitor; a peculiar old man who appeared on the porch one day, and then was there ever after every time we came. He mumbled, repeatedly, but we never could catch what he was saying. He was, nonetheless, the source of our information about the house. We read the whole story in brittle newspaper clippings he left for us on one of his visits, clippings which told how the house was haunted by the noises of the highway. The news saddened us, and when, finally, the time came for us to spend our first night there, we were not a little apprehensive. We settled in, and we listened, but we felt no rumblings, heard no sounds of traffic, no screams. We speculate that the years of standing with windows and doors open had let the pent up sounds out of the house. But to this day, that old man is on our front porch, saying again and again, "*You don't want that house.*"

There's an old man on a bench, a ghost in plaid shirt and suspenders. You wonder if he is stubborn, or if ghosts cannot change their minds.

He looks at you in a conspiratorial way, as if he is going to say something, but once again you find yourself somewhere else, with no say in the matter. You are back in the main gallery, in front of the door to that house, a door with a name on it: Hillside House. You want to protest that you don't seem to have any better control over what you experience here in The Gallery Pitu than you do at home with the interactive TV and its clumsy controls. When you look around, you find that you are alone, except for voices coming from a box near the plate glass window. When you step a bit closer, you can hear that someone is interviewing the artist, whose voice has been disguised through some sort of computer distortion.

"Is it possible for you to have friends?" the interviewer asks, sounding worried that the artist might not have any. "I mean, if you snoop, who can trust you?"

"Oh," replies the false voice of the artist, "one only spies on strangers."

"Why is that?"

"With someone you care about, you never want to learn something you'd be happier not knowing. The Bluebeard Effect, you know."

Interviewer: "Of course."

With a shudder, you walk away from the box, look for an exhibit you'd choose to enter.

The first thing you notice is a spot on the exhibition wall that is all but empty, as if the artist had gone away in the middle of hanging the work. There are, held by tacks, two ratty scraps of paper, one with words: my elder sister. The other has scribbled on it a rough musical score. Reading it, you try to hear it in your head. Possibly you hum a note?

My Elder Sister

My elder sister was the wildest of all the girls. Her long, smooth legs flashed brown as she ran, faster than all the others, faster than the boys. Faster, running silently with the deer. I believed I saw her running with the deer, and not in a dream. I was the smallest of the children then, more than a baby, but small enough that someone would carry me if I got too tired to walk. Our elder brothers were already old enough to hunt, but they, too, played games with us, the games of following trails, of stalking one another, carrying small bows. Some would put animal skins over their backs. The rest of us would hunt them.

My sister, the wildest of all the girls, also went

with the girls and women to pick berries. Her long, slender fingers were as quick and careful as the blink of an eye. Oh, she could fill her baskets! But how our mother scolded her for her wildness.

"Watch!" our mother would say. "Watch for the scats of the bears. If you see them, don't race over them. Stop. Look. Are they old? Are they fresh? Do you want to meet the bears who are picking berries? Do you dare to mock the bear? A hunter may risk mocking a bear. The hunter may kill the bear or be killed by the bear, but you! By mocking the bear you draw attention to yourself."

Our mother scolded, but still my elder sister raced, leapt, laughing lightly, a breeze past me; and always, when I asked her, my sister sang for me.

I, a small boy who believed that he would someday grow up to be a hunter, I practiced tracking. I studied the trails, looked and looked at the scats of deer, mice, gophers, bears, and the middens beneath a tree, which show where squirrels have food. I tracked my brothers and my sister. I grew bigger and stronger, but I was still too young for the hunt when I tracked my sister and the others as they picked berries. When the baskets were full, I was still eating, the last one at the berry patch. My sister went ahead of me on the path, she, too, far behind the others. My sister, who never stumbled, did just then, spilling some of her berries. I hurried to catch up to her, to help her, when a tall young man, strong, the handsome man I dreamed I would be someday, stepped out from behind a tree and said something to my elder sister. She stood up, the basket in her hand, and looked at him. He put the palm of his hand gently on her forehead, his fingers on her black hair. He bowed his head; she bowed hers.

When he took his hand away from her head, I could see that my sister had no memory, no thought of me behind her on the path, nor any memory of the others ahead of her. She had forgotten her family. Then my elder sister took the man's hand, and together they walked away.

Though I wanted to cry out to them, I somehow knew I must not, nor did I ever tell what I had seen. My sister had done a strange thing, to marry a stranger and walk away from us. I hoped that I would see her again, but I believed that she had gone forever.

Days passed. First the nights and then the days grew colder. I dreamed my sister and her husband walked far, far.

Winter came and went, and another summer warmed us before the cold came again. I had grown, but still was not old enough to hunt, though I tracked the hunters often enough, and was allowed to help them on the homeward trip.

My sister and her husband did walk far, far. And then, after a time, they returned to places near to us. As they walked and talked, my sister's husband was a handsome man, tall and brave, strong and gentle. But my elder sister saw that when her husband went to hunt, he was a bear. When they returned to a place near to us, my elder sister's family, my sister recognized the places, remembered the places.

Her husband said that winter was coming and they must make a den. My sister, who walked slowly because the time was near for her to give birth, agreed. Her husband told her to bring branches and boughs for their den. Then, becoming a bear, he began to dig a place into the hillside. My sister, as the time for giving birth was so close, remembered us, longed for us, her family. She thought that she could bring her two families together. My elder sister thought that if her family could see her husband the fine man, they would not kill her husband the bear. My sister took boughs for the den, but she also rubbed her body with leaves, rubbed her body with sand, rubbed against the bark of trees, to fill them with her scent. She took boughs from high on the trees, leaving traces that marked her passing. Then she went to the den, walking slowly. After her husband had completed the den, he walked around outside that place, and he saw where my elder sister had broken the branches. He smelled the scent of my elder sister on the leaves and pine needles, and he returned to the den, saying, "We must leave this place. Your brothers will find us here and then I must kill them."

"No," cried my elder sister. "They are your brothers-in-law. You must not kill them. You must never kill members of your family."

"Then we must leave," said the bear who was my sister's husband.

Slowly, my sister followed her husband to a new place, where once again he began to dig into the hillside. Once again my sister helped to make a comfortable den. Once again my sister marked the place, so longing to be together with her family, so sure that she could make peace between her brothers and her husband. This time, she was more careful, but still her husband saw the traces. He sighed, but said nothing, and they moved into the den. There they spent the long winter. My sister sang for her husband. He told her many stories, taught her many secrets. He turned from man to bear to man and to bear again, a shaman of beauty, power, and kindness. My elder sister gave birth that winter to two babies, a boy and a girl. And then the day came when my sister's husband said, "The hunters, your brothers, are coming. They will find the traces you have left. I must go to kill them or they will kill me." My sister begged him not to kill her brothers, for they were family. She was certain that if he would only show himself as a man to her brothers, then all would go well for them. But my sister's husband, though he spoke to her like a human, looked, in those last days, like a bear.

Shaking his great shaggy head, he said to her, "After they kill me, ask them to give you my skull and my tail. Make a fire, and burn them until they are completely consumed. While they burn, you must sing this song." There, in the den, he stood to teach her the song that she must sing. My sister learned the song, but thought always that if he would only show himself to her brothers as a human, then everything would go well for them.

On the last day, the barking of hunting dogs on the scent of bear awoke my sister and her husband. My sister's husband went out of the den, leaving my sister and her babies inside. My tracking of the hunters brought me to them after my elder brothers had killed the great bear that was my sister's husband. From that place, we could hear our sister singing her mourning song. We knew her voice. "Go," my elder brothers said to me. "Smallest brother. Go to our sister. You have not killed."

I went to where my sister was inside her den, singing her song of mourning. She said that our brothers must give her the skull and tail of the great bear, and that I must make a fire for her. "Then go home and ask our mother to make a dress for me, and for my baby daughter, and pants and shirt for my son, and moccasins for us. Bring them here tomorrow so that we may come back to our family." I did as she had told me, but took no part in the feast that night. I dreamed I saw my elder sister as she stood by the fire, singing the song her husband had taught her, the one he had asked her to sing while the fire consumed his skull and tail.

The next day I took the clothing to my sister. When she had dressed herself and her children, we started the long walk back to our mother and our brothers.

"Please help me," my sister asked as we approached the place. "The smell of humans is too strong for me. Help me make a camp a bit away, so that I can become accustomed to the smell gradually."

I helped my sister make a camp. She and her children lived there all summer, and I near to them. Our brothers called her the Widow of the Bear, and listened sometimes when she sang or told stories she had learned from her husband. I held her children, played with them, fed them, but our brothers were cold to them. From my sister that summer, I learned songs, stories, the stories of their journey, and secrets her husband told that winter in their den.

The time came when our brothers went out again to hunt. I did not go with them, but listened to the stories my sister told. Our brothers came back with a bear, a mother bear dead and two live cubs. There was a feast, and the song of the bear was sung, with the skull and tail consumed by fire. There was some grumbling from our elder brothers the hunters. How could their younger sister be so bold as to claim she knew what they must do? That night, while the others slept, my sister told me how to find two mother bears in their dens, mothers with only one cub born that winter. My sister told me how to trick the mothers into accepting the orphan cubs. My sister said that we had meat aplenty, and that grown bears would be better for the hunters than the meat of these cubs. I did as my sister told.

In the days that followed, our elder brothers did not mention the cubs. They played instead the hunting games with the bear skin. My sister's babies had grown large enough to run about with the other children, on two feet, laughing and playing, but my sister would not let them play the bear game, would not play the bear game with our brothers.

"Mother," she begged our mother. "Mother, please tell our brothers not to play that game with us. See the hair on my arms and legs? If they play that game with me I'll become a bear. I felt it already happening to me when I lived with my husband that last winter in our den."

"You?" our mother said. "You, who were always too bold, now you want me to order them not to play a harmless game? Teach your children."

Again and again our brothers taunted my elder sister, saying, "You. You who ran with the deer. Now you are moving more slowly, like the mother bear. Come. Come play the bear game with us. You who used to laugh so much. Come."

Again our sister begged our mother to help.

At last our brothers, laughing and whispering, sneaked up behind our sister and her children. Our laughing elder brothers were followed by all the little children, bearing tiny bows in their small fists. Our laughing brothers threw bearskins over my elder sister and her children, and I saw her children, and my sister, become bears.

Two cubs, my sister's children, ran away. My sister, weeping all the while, killed our elder brothers and our mother, and then, the tears running down her face, she ran after her cubs into the mountains. From that time, I sing the songs my sister taught me, and the one about her love, and her hopes, and her sorrows. The people hunt other bears, but not the one called — but only with great courtesy — the Grizzly, for that bear is half human.

The younger brother of the woman who became a bear ends his song and walks away from you, into the forest. You start after him, to follow him, to learn the song, but find yourself pulled away, pulled back, back into the gallery.

Maybe you should just go home, forget about this place. But you are stubborn, determined that you will choose an exhibit and not be trapped into one.

At the end of the gallery is a window that looks out on a garden choked with weeds and brambles. Turning from the window, you peer around to see what exhibits are on the other side of the center partition. As you do, out of the corner of your eye, you notice something funny about that garden. When you look back, you see a new fence has cut off your view. It looks about six feet tall, made of fresh wood nailed very close together. There is no gate, but

*pointed slats nailed all around. Why the fence?
Has something in the garden changed so that
someone wants to cut off the view? You step
closer, tempted to climb it. Suddenly the fence
is gone. The garden is magnificent: flowers,
trees, birds, a fountain, a bench. It's incredible
how different it looks. There is a house in the
garden. You decide to take a closer look. Yes, if
this is an exhibit (and you think it must be),
then it is one you choose. You open the window.
Abruptly, the fence is back. At first you think
it must be some sort of laser display or one of
those angled reflections, where an eye has been
painted onto glass or plastic. The eye is open
from one angle, but closed from another. By
walking backward you can make the eye blink
or wink. To test it, you reach for the fence, not
at all sure you won't be sucked away somewhere, but, no. The fence is solid; real wood,
and solid. To see what is behind it, you must
climb.*

*When you do, you find yourself being
squished, made smaller and smaller, so that by
the time you are at the top, you fly through that
garden, into the house, no choice in the matter;
you are a fly on the wall. At first it is a bit
confusing to see and hear as a fly does, but after
a while you begin to understand.*

The Coffeepot

Rhoda Greene had been all her life a person solitary. She was a middle-sized person living in a middle-sized town in the middle of the country. There, alone in her middle-sized house, she did her work, which was to write and draw picture books for small children. Rhoda Greene's books were the sort that children found pleasant and grown-ups found reassuring. Rhoda worked with oils, paper collages, pastels, inks, and sometimes watercolors, which are far more difficult to do well than most people imagine.

Rhoda did leave her house two afternoons a week, to work in the town library. The children, who visited the library in large numbers, liked Rhoda, in part because she hired them to answer her fan mail. A kid who worked for Rhoda

Greene took home a stack of letters and wrote whatever sort of reply he or she wanted. Rhoda paid for postage, paper, and for the time it took to do the job. She trusted kids to write more interesting letters than she would, and to tell her when they had outgrown the job. For more than twenty-five years, kids had been writing letters for Rhoda.

Rhoda spent her free time alone, gardening. Many people dream of having a garden like Rhoda's. Some people try.

One thing that Rhoda Greene did not do, and never ever did, was cook. Rhoda disliked cooking with such intensity, and was so indifferent to food, that she never even made pictures of cookies or tea parties, not so much as a glass of milk, in any of her books. For her own sustenance, she ate absentmindedly: dry bread, crackers, double vitamins, whatever came to hand.

In like manner, she absentmindedly took a cup of coffee now and again while she was at her drawing board. Trouble was, she'd set the kettle to boil, or the pot to perk, and then lose herself in her drawing or in her gardening. She had burned up a considerable number of teakettles and kitchen pans while attempting to boil water for a cup of instant. Of course, Rhoda had noticed that she burned those pots, and had tried all sorts of devices, including electric kettles that turned themselves off when they had boiled dry. Even those kettles had eventually burned out. And somehow coffee makers did not work for Rhoda. She forgot to put in the water or the coffee or to plug them in or to turn them off. Whatever. If Rhoda had lived in the right sort of town, she could have had coffee delivered, or depended on a favorite nearby coffee house, or something; but no such luck where Rhoda lived.

Well, it happened that after Rhoda Greene had been working at the library for twenty years or more, the others with whom she worked learned that Rhoda only got a decent cup of coffee on the two days a week she worked there, and they learned why. Without a second thought, they appointed one of their number to find an appropriate coffee maker for poor, dear Rhoda. Having found just the one, they bought it and gave it to her, crying, "Surprise!"

Rhoda *was* surprised, astonished in fact. She thanked them, then took the box containing the machine out to her car. When she got back home, she followed the single instruction that came with the machine, plugging its cord into the outlet just above the tiny counter in her tiny kitchen.

"Good day to you," said the coffeepot.

Rhoda was a bit startled. The machine continued, "Please fill the receptacle with cold water up to the line indicated. Waiting. Waiting. Waiting — "

The machine continued repeating the word *waiting* until Rhoda had done as she had been instructed.

Rhoda felt a small but definite twinge of dislike for this coffeepot. The machine, however, continued to instruct Rhoda until she had measured the coffee and put it into the machine. It then told her to go about her business until it called her for a cup of fine, delicious . . . Rhoda left the room before the machine finished its sentence.

She went to her drawing board, but found she could not concentrate. Having that thing in the kitchen was like having a person in the house, impossible to work. Rhoda tidied up her work area, sharpened pencils, looked out the window. She walked outside to remove a single dead leaf from a geranium plant and crumple it into the compost heap. It was dark and not very warm outside, no time to garden, not even for Rhoda.

Uneasy, Rhoda drifted back to the house. She could hear the machine calling to her, announcing that the coffee was perfectly brewed, piping hot, etcetera, etcetera. Rhoda's ears blazed red. She did not want anyone or anything telling her that coffee or anything else was perfectly anything. The machine kept talking, and Rhoda felt she'd have no peace until she poured a cup. She poured, pulling out the plug on the machine as she did. Rhoda did not give a hoot whether her coffee was kept hot or not.

Late that night, Rhoda sat down with the wiring guide for the coffee maker. She read every diagram with great care. When she had finished, she set to work to deprogram the coffee pot. She took out the microchip that contained the talking part of the machine. Yes, she knew that her kindly coworkers had bought the machine just because it talked; they had wanted to give her a machine that she could not burn up. But Rhoda much preferred burning a pot to listening to one. Once she had finished removing from the pot the possibility that it could talk to her, Rhoda went to bed, leaving the coffee maker unplugged, turned off, sitting in the dark on the tiny counter in her tiny kitchen. Rhoda went to bed muttering that she'd *make* coffee and *drink* coffee when she wanted, not when ordered.

Just before sunrise, Rhoda jolted awake. She took a deep breath, lay there blinking up at the ceiling, trying to collect her scattered thoughts, trying to still the thumping of her heart. It must have been a nightmare, that voice ordering her to get up, to get to that drawing board, to clean the refrigerator. In the nightmare there had been the smell of coffee. She still smelled it, not bad smelling, but pungent. Rhoda sat up, then stood up, and walked over to close the bedroom window. It was real. In the cold fresh air of the bedroom she could smell warm little currents of coffee-laden air. Rhoda listened.

"Rhoda. Let us remember, the early bird catches the worm. Coffee is ready. Time to go to work. Books don't write themselves, you know." Rhoda dashed down the stairs. The machine, full of dark, steaming coffee, was plugged into the wall outlet above her kitchen counter. "Very funny," muttered Rhoda, unplugging the machine. She could not think of anyone she knew who had that sort of humor, but then the gift of the machine from the library people had been a surprise, after all. And who would think to set the yak yak of the machine so that it talked directly to Rhoda?

Rhoda sighed. Can't hurt to drink the coffee, can't hurt to get to work, either. Rhoda, who did not want to hear what other wonderful, witty things the machine had to say, checked once more that it was, indeed, unplugged, then went into her study and flicked on the lights.

Rhoda worked rather well that day, and in the days that followed, though she never could find out who came into the house every night to fill the machine and plug it in. Rhoda removed and threw out the microchip, deprogrammed the talking, unplugged the machine every morning after she had poured her coffee and checked it before she went to bed each night, and still the machine made coffee and babbled cheerful, bossy nonsense at her. When Rhoda asked her coworkers, they looked quite convincingly bewildered and, finally, amused. They claimed to think that she, Rhoda Greene, was pulling their legs.

At night Rhoda was dreaming some pretty odd stuff. She could see that her little adventure with the coffeepot was having its effect on her work. Her publisher telephoned.

"Rhoda Dear!" came the usual cheerful, loud voice. "New phase? I mean, dear, your work sells so well. Why tamper with what is successful?"

Rhoda said nothing, waiting for the publisher to get to the point.

"These drawings. Charming. Funny. Some say delightful, but so different from what I love about your work. The eyes. It's the eyes of the children. They are so watchful. Rhoda Dear, are you listening?"

Rhoda Greene shifted the telephone to her other ear. "If you don't want the book — "

"No, dear. Of course I want the book. But . . ." The publisher sighed. Parents and librarians had come to expect those reassuring books. This one was somehow not so reassuring. It would be a risk. The publisher could and did trim the risk by planning to print fewer copies of the new book than she would normally do. With a small prayer for luck, she began to prepare a new contract for Rhoda. All the while, she was hoping that Rhoda would regain her good sense and not pursue this peculiar new style.

The coffee maker grew daily more talkative. Furthermore, it woke Rhoda earlier each morning, and said "tisk tisk" at her when she left her drawing board to go into the garden. No wonder the eyes of the children in Rhoda's books looked watchful. Rhoda felt watched.

The day came when the machine said chattily, "You know, Rhoda Greene, you really ought to learn to cook. It is a failure on your part not to know how to cook." Upon those words, Rhoda picked up the coffee maker, carried it directly to the Salvation Army box and deposited it there. She attached a note saying, *This coffee maker makes good coffee, but it is programmed to talk. For me, the talk is unpleasant. Hope it is not for someone else. Good Luck.*"

With a sigh of relief, Rhoda Greene went home to her house and garden and enjoyed a quiet day, the first in weeks.

The library staff witnessed what happened next. It was just past closing time, the room full of that pleasant fatigue people feel at the end of a good day: The job is done; it will feel good to go home, put up your feet, relax. The staff refreshment area was clean, a task they took turns doing. The coffee maker, a solid, silent old model that had been there for years, had been washed, dried, unplugged. The cups and spoons were clean in the cupboard; sugar, milk, all stored safely away. Rhoda and five others were collecting their belongings when a voice demanded: "Rhoda Greene. Go fetch your coffee maker immediately. Go get it this minute. Waste not; want not, Rhoda Greene!"

Rhoda, ashen faced, stared at the place from which the voice had come, the staff room coffee maker. The others, all but one, stood thunderstruck. That one, a woman in sensible shoes, picked up the offending coffee maker and carried it out the door. Without hesitating, she walked directly to the metal/plastic recycling can, and opened it. She put the coffee maker, which was still talking, into the can and closed the lid. That lady then walked back into the staff room and offered to walk Rhoda home. Rhoda said quite firmly that she would be fine, thank you, and left. The others quickly departed, each in his or her separate direction.

The lady in sensible shoes was troubled by what had happened, and did not sleep well that night.

It was altogether peculiar. The very next day, the library received a letter saying that Rhoda Greene resigned from the staff. Rhoda had been a solitary person, so after a week had gone by, her colleagues did not expect to hear Rhoda's voice on the phone or see Rhoda at the door, just for a visit. No one was waiting to be invited over for dinner or coffee or tea or to pull taffy.

Still, they missed her. She had been a good worker, good company. The lady in sensible shoes was concerned. She telephoned, but got only a recording, which said that Ms. Greene was away on a business trip, the house rented, and no solicitation permitted.

Rhoda's bills were paid. Her house was lit at night; but the garden, poor thing, fell to wrack and ruin. In no time at all it was choked with weeds and vines, grew dense and dark. Tattered bits of plastic and shreds of paper stuck to the brambles, shards of glass glittered in the refuse that collected along the edge of the weeds. It became an altogether dismal spot.

The publisher received manuscripts, which were increasingly strange, but immensely successful as books. The publisher was in heaven, had to hire a staff to answer huge bags of fan mail. The old books still sold, because they reassured parents; the new books were read by an entirely different group of children. Critics described them glowingly as "capturing the poignant paranoia of childhood."

During the weeks and months that passed, the lady in sensible shoes continued to feel troubled about the departure of Rhoda Greene. For one thing, that lady loved and cared for a garden of her own, and she'd walked past Rhoda's house and she'd seen the tangle at Rhoda's. It made her feel sad.

The lady in sensible shoes respected Rhoda's desire for privacy, but nevertheless had gone once to the house and rung the bell. But no one answered. She then wrote a note, but got no reply. At last, she put on her gardening gloves, her mackintosh to guard against thorns and stickers, and went to see what was happening at the house of Rhoda Greene.

It took some time to make her way through the undergrowth, but at last the lady in sensible shoes managed to get to the house, to circle it until she found a cracked pane in one of the windows. There was so much talking going on inside the house that she was able to put a piece of tape against the cracked pane and pull until the glass came out. Then she could put her gloved hand very carefully through the place where the glass had been and push aside the window shade, hoping all the time that the shade would not suddenly roll itself up and reveal her prowling.

The lady in sensible shoes gasped when she saw poor Rhoda Greene. She stood in the kitchen, on a leash made of electrical cord, stirring something in a saucepan on the front left burner of the stove. On each of the other burners something was cooking. While the lady in sensible shoes watched, horrified, poor Rhoda chopped and stirred, sautéed, whipped, dipped, and deglazed pans. She cooked, cooked, cooked, while voices directed, berated, scolded, bossed her without pause. The refrigerator's tone was almost kindly, but not so the stove, the vacuum cleaner, the very light bulbs. The ringleader, the coffeepot, sneered from the tiny kitchen counter.

"After your cooking lesson, it's back to the drawing board for you, Rhoda Greene. After all, rest makes rust. And we don't want you all rusty." The laughter that followed made the lady in sensible shoes weak with terror. What if the coffeepot saw her? Could it know that she never cooked if she could help it, that she had thrown the library coffeepot into the recycling bin? What could she do? She wanted to rescue Rhoda Greene, not join her.

You, the fly on the wall, with your many eyes, see the fear on the face of the lady in sensible shoes as she peers in the window. You buzz with agitation and a measure of sympathy for poor Rhoda. It was a mistake, for the coffeepot notices you and says, "And later on, when you have finished your other duties, Rhoda Greene, you will sit down with a mail-order catalog and order a fine electronic insect zapper. We cannot tolerate vermin such as that nasty fly on the wall."

Quicker than a human eye can blink, you wing it up and out of there, away from danger, until you find yourself buzzing lazy circles in the late-afternoon light that filters through the largish plate-glass window of The Gallery Pitu. A metallic voice is repeating a message: "The gallery is closing. The gallery is closing. It is closing time at The Gallery Pitu."

All at once, the gallery, which has been empty every time you have seen it, is filled with people, some talking of the exhibits. You hear "voyeur," and "thrill of discovery," and "Imagine: There is always the chance that you will find an incident from your own life right here!" Other visitors creep out the door, looking always behind them as if expecting something unpleasant.

With a thump, you are on the floor, sitting there, no longer a fly, but a human once again, embarrassed to be dropped like that in a heap, but no one notices. You pick yourself up, saunter out. You have been a fly, spying on the lady in sensible shoes, who was spying on her friend, the artist having spied on all of them, and possibly on you. You go home, tired beyond belief. At dinner that night, you are very quiet, afterward going straight to bed, exhausted, but sure that tomorrow you will return to The Gallery Pitu. There were things you never got close to seeing.

The next morning when you awake, the weather is mild, but your parents are not. You must take care of your younger sister, all day. Normally, you would not mind. Your sister is okay, and admires you greatly, but she is an outdoor child. It will not be easy to convince her to join you on a visit to The Gallery Pitu. She likes the park, which is empty when you arrive. You settle on 653 as the number of times you must push her in the swing before she will go with you into The Gallery Pitu. Others arrive in the park, small children in strollers pushed by young people reading folded newspapers as they walk, chess and checker players, and a bearded young man with one gold earring, a red bandanna knotted around his blond ponytail. He is carrying what appears to be a guitar case. He sits down on one of the empty benches, opens the case, takes out a guitar, then closes the case and puts it behind him on the bench. An open case means that a musician is playing to earn money. What does it mean to play with the case closed? The young man strums softly, strums and sings so quietly that it is as if he is playing for himself. Your little sister relinquishes her swing at 437 pushes, walks over to where she can observe the young man. By the time he pauses in his playing, your little sister is standing quite close to him.

"What language was that?" she asks.

"A dialect of the Faeroe Islands, a kind of old Viking language," he replies.

"How do you know it?"

"I was born there."

"Will you go back?"

"Tomorrow."

"This park will miss you."

"Yes."

Your little sister turns away from the young man and comes to where you are standing by the swing, which is once again empty. No. She shakes her head. She will not hold you to the 653 pushes, but says she is ready to visit The Gallery Pitu.

You ring the bell; the buzzer responds. The door opens.

Your little sister holds your hand as the two of you walk inside. Once again, the gallery is empty. Today you want to see the exhibits on the left of the central partition, the ones you missed yesterday. When you step in that direction, your little sister at first pulls to the right, then changes her mind when she sees a gray cat sitting next to the wall toward which you had been heading. She crouches to visit with the cat, which seems to be quite affectionate, purring and rubbing against her. Your little sister sits down, her back resting against the gray wall of the gallery. The cat climbs into her lap. Until this moment, you had refused to think of what you would do with your sister once inside The Gallery Pitu. But now, with the cat, she seems safe enough. Surely you can look and not touch anything. Your parents would be justifiably annoyed with you should you fail to take good care of your little sister. You absolutely will not take part in any exhibit. Today is strictly for having an overview, just to see what is here.

Maybe it won't even be interesting enough to be worth another visit.

Hands clasped behind your back, you stroll down the center of the aisle. Right and left are exhibits. It's odd how the artist seems obsessed with maps. You had not noticed yesterday, but today you see, one after another, maps as part of the works of art. You shrug. Of course, if the artist follows strangers, then the artist must go to unknown places, and once there, must need a map to find the way home.

A map of Austin, Texas.

Another. It says: Damascus.

That one is of some wilderness, a woods in the far north. You look back. Your little sister and the gray cat are nose to nose, as if deep in conversation.

Next to the north woods map is a group of photographs, an almanac, thick books. You can't see the titles. On the floor, there is a key. Without thinking that it might be part of the exhibit, you stoop down, pick it up, trying to read the smudged ink on the paper tag attached to it. You read "Moon," then something illegible, just before you feel yourself once again sliding, sliding, into a place where someone is helpless with fear.

Moonpath

Until last night, Roddy had a best friend.

Three weeks ago, Roddy's parents had driven a whole day through dense forest to reach the cabin. Roddy's mother had unlocked the door, saying that the boys should choose which bedroom they'd like.

Without hesitation, Roddy and his best friend had carried their sleeping bags into the tiny room with the huge windows at the foot of the bed, two windows facing Moon Lake.

For 21 days Roddy and his best friend — Roddy cannot bear to say his name — hiked in the mountains, swam, canoed, and fished in Moon Lake. They had built their own lean-to in the woods, cooked on their own camp fire, quarreled and made up. And now Roddy's best friend is gone, and Roddy's parents have not even noticed.

The almost-full moon came up last night,

golden in the evening sky. Later Roddy awoke to see the moon's face silver above the mountains behind the opposite shore, the moon's path golden on Moon Lake. The path shone, shimmered, rippled across the lake into Roddy's room, clear up the sleeping bag next to Roddy's. Roddy's best friend stirred, sat up. The expression on his face gave Roddy chills. Roddy reached out to restrain his best friend. "Wait! I'll close the curtains." But Roddy's friend, his eyes pure silver, pushed Roddy's hand away. Rising, he stepped onto his shimmering sleeping bag, then ran along the golden moonpath until he disappeared into the silver face of the moon high above Moon Lake.

During the hours of bright daylight, Roddy dreaded the coming night and the round, powerful, compelling moon.

Now, night has come. Roddy walks over to close the curtains, only to find that they are gone. "Oh," his mother says lightly. "I washed them, then forgot to take them in, so they're wet with dew. They'll be back up tomorrow."

Yesterday Roddy had a best friend. Now, in his sleeping bag, Roddy waits for the moonpath to reach him, and knows that tomorrow morning his parents will not even notice.

The Other Side of the Moon

Josiah was an "only-est" child. That was the word he made up to describe his condition. It was not simply that Josiah was an only child, or that he was the only child of parents who were much, much older than anyone would ever expect parents of an eleven-year-old boy to be. Josiah was the only child of elderly parents whose work caused the family to move rather often and to live in places one could modestly describe as remote.

Josiah's scholarly parents studied mosses and lichens. Josiah's parents were kindly, often witty, and they were generous. When Josiah was very little, they lived for a short time in a house that had a television set. Josiah, who even then longed for a playmate, saw a toy on the television that seemed to be just what he needed. There, on the television, Josiah could see children in a friendly group, all enjoying a wonderful, delightful, most desirable toy together!

After Josiah's parents gave him that toy, after Josiah had that toy all to himself for a full day, Josiah realized that he had been tricked by the television, and was never fooled that way again.

Years passed. Josiah and his parents drove from one wilderness spot to another, spending weeks here, months or even a year there. Josiah took his lessons at home, or at a school if there was one nearby. He did a great many things alone, and did a great many things with his parents, and enjoyed what he did. Mostly, he was content. Still, Josiah knew he'd rather not be an only-est child.

One hot day in July, Josiah and his parents drove through dense forest to a small village. It would take another hour of driving to reach the cabin they'd rented. Josiah did not mind cabins, and he most definitely liked lakes. A cabin on a lake in July could be promising. There might be lots of kids there. You never knew. Then Josiah heard the agent who gave them the keys say, "It's the only cabin on Moon Lake, a beautiful spot."

* * *

For himself, Josiah chose a tiny bedroom with two huge windows looking out on the lake. An old-fashioned double bed with an ornate metal headboard nearly filled the room. It was a bed fine for sleeping, fine for reading. For three weeks, Josiah fished and swam, canoed, hiked, and read. Sometimes he and his parents sailed the ratty little boat that came with the cabin. In those three weeks, they never saw a single person on Moon Lake.

Then, one night when the moon was almost full, Josiah awoke to see the silver moon high above the mountains beyond the opposite shore. Josiah could see that from the moon, straight across Moon Lake, came a broad golden path shimmering, shining right through the windows and right up his sleeping bag. Josiah sat up. That path made his heart pound just to look at it. Josiah sat and stared.

On the path, a figure walked, then ran toward him. It was a boy, whose eyes shone silver when he first arrived, but quieted to a regular dark brown once he got accustomed to the dark. Josiah and the boy talked away the better part of the night, and when they fell asleep, Josiah had a friend.

The next morning, when the two boys appeared at breakfast, Josiah's parents did not seem the least bit surprised.

That night, the night of the full moon, Josiah and his friend were sound asleep in their sleeping bags when once again the bright moonlight reached across the lake into their room. Both boys awoke, and watched a dark figure walk, then run, along the golden moonpath into their room.

In the morning, Josiah had two friends; his father made more pancakes.

The following night, the bed was crowded with three sleeping bags, and the moon was on the wane, when one more boy walked and then ran down the path into the room.

The next day, Josiah's parents said the lichen work was done for now on Moon Lake. They packed their gear, then closed the cabin. For ever more, Josiah and his three best friends, who lived together and grew up as if they were brothers, wondered: If they had stayed at the cabin any longer, would Josiah's parents have needed to buy a bigger car? Or, would the moon have taken all the boys up the golden path into the silver moon?

Back in The Gallery Pitu, the key falls from your hand, clatters as it hits the wooden floor. You are no longer afraid with one boy, nor glad with the others, but desperate. Where is your little sister? Did she stay safely with the cat, or did she touch something? You race around the corner. No sign of her. The cat is washing its face with its right front paw. It turns to meow at you as you run past. A second room? How could you have missed seeing it yesterday? You run down one side of the central partition, back up the other, panting. What can you do? There is nobody to ask. If she has gone into an exhibit, surely she will be out, safely out, soon. Won't she? Your palms icy and dripping with sweat, you look for the gray cat, first in the new room, then back in what you think of as the main room. The cat, too, is gone. Across the street, the park is empty.

"I'm hungry. Can we have lunch?"

You jump. "Where were you?"

She shrugs, "With the kittens."

"Oh. I got scared when I didn't see you."

"Why? The place is empty. It's not as if you could lose me," replies your sensible little sister. Taking your hand, she waves good-bye to the gray cat, which has reappeared.

"No guest book to sign?" your little sister asks, glancing around the entrance door.

"I don't know if I want to leave our address," you reply.

"What do you want to do after lunch?" asks your little sister.

"Oh, I dunno."

"I'd like to go back there. The farm and the kittens were fun," she replies.

You make no answer. She's little. She might have sat there petting the cat, imagining all sorts of things, being on a farm and whatnot. But, then, maybe the cat, too, was part of an exhibit.

You did not touch it, have no idea where it might have led. You decide to be prudent, spend the afternoon at a different park. You'll offer your little sister a less risky activity. Yes. You'll tempt her with her favorite pastime: you as goalie in front of a soccer net, she kicking soccer balls at the goal until she drops from exhaustion.

* * *

The following morning you awaken, once more free to go alone to The Gallery Pitu. Rain falls in a fine mist. The park, its benches, sidewalk, grass, and leaves glistening wet, is empty. Inside, the gallery is chilly, unpleasantly still. Your breath makes steam clouds. It would be nice to be somewhere warm. You are wondering if any exhibit offers that option when you stumble over something on the floor, a tool for tightening trucks on a . . .

Off the Wall

Skateboard. You are holding a beat-up old board under one arm, an unblemished new one, wheels humming, ready to go, under your other arm. You are you but inside someone, which is totally strange. You see and think and feel like this person, but at the same time are watching him. The person is Jason, a stocky guy; the muscles feeling different from your own. Jason is walking with his best friend, Albert, a pale tall skinny kid, who also is carrying an old board and a new one.

You are walking, and not riding on these awesome new boards because of the two old ladies walking behind you. They are your grandmothers, and they are strict. They are "please" and "thank you" grandmothers. Jason's grandmother is short and stocky, Al's is long and lean.

You live with your grandmother, and Al lives with his; and the two grandmothers are best friends. They drink tea and talk about books, and they take long walks, and they will stop perfect strangers on the street to remind them to pick up a piece of trash just dropped. They police the world, your grandmothers do.

You are walking because of the sign on Main Street which says, NO BIKES OR SKATEBOARDS ON THE SIDEWALK. Your grandmothers have just come from the Y, where they take some exercise class together. Well, actually, they take a martial art — Tae Kwon Do — and in fact they are wearing their white cotton uniforms out on the street because a flood in the locker room had made it impossible to change back into their regular grandmother clothes. You and your friend are a bit embarrassed to have them out in public in those white pajama-looking clothes, and to make it worse, it does not seem to bother the old ladies at all. They even offered to treat you to ice cream. You and your friend are torn. You would love to dip into a fine ice cream. But here you are with new boards, bought today after saving your money from months and months of hard work. You want to escape to ride the boards over at the abandoned gas station. Then, when you are chased away from *that* lot, you can go to the library, until you are chased away, and then to the college, and then . . . and then. All the world loves a lover, but nobody loves a skateboarder.

Here, on the street near the bank, would be a terrific spot, with these stone benches and the smooth sidewalk and those miles of cement buffers lining the flower beds. You could do some awesome skating here. There are steps, garbage cans to ollie over, everything you need to skate. But it can never happen, not with grandmothers and rules and. . . . You look at your friend. Both of you sigh. You could come once at dawn, before the stores and bank are open. That's what all the skaters in California do. That's when they make their homemade videos. If you had a camera you could film your friend, and he you.

You dream. Then, *wham*, a huge guy smashes out of a fancy shop next to the bank. He slams past, hitting you with a load of clothes on heavy hangers, as he dashes for a van double-parked on Main Street. From the shop door, someone shouts, "Stop! Thief!"

You drop your old board, jump down on your new one, race after the guy. Behind you, your grandmother says, "See here. That was rude." She grabs your old board, sends it right for the thief's ankles. *Wham*, down he goes, the clothes fly up into the air. You execute a fine rail slide along the concrete, and catch an armload of clothes. And there, right behind you, your grandmother jumps onto the still-moving old board, skates, catches herself an armload, skates on, then does a quite incredible especially-for-an-old-lady smooth turn and stop.

You cannot take time to admire her because two masked guys are running out of the bank, each with a gun and a canvas bag. They wave the guns, snarl for everybody to "get outta the way." Al's grandmother steps toward them, saying, "You there, sirrah! Take that bag, and you too," pointing her finger at the other robber. "Take those bags right back where they belong. This instant!"

When the robbers ignore her, the old lady turns to your friend, hand outstretched, saying, "Albert?" He hands her one board, jumps on the other. In parallel, Al and his grandmother skate low and fast, past the robbers, grabbing the bags of money with an upward swing that knocks the pistols flying through the air. Your friend and his grandmother then skate in a big curve right back through the doors of the bank. Suddenly, the police are everywhere, arresting angry robbers. You look at your grandmother, who smiles at you. You skate fast, pick up speed, jump, slide along a bench, curve down, stop. Your friend skates out of the bank. A moment later out his grandmother walks, carrying her board.

There is ice cream, and photos in the newspaper, and the bank puts up a statue of a skateboarder, right next to the sign that says NO . . .

You, plain old you in your own body, but all sweaty and with hands and face sticky with ice cream, and a thirst in your throat that kills; you are back in the gallery. There must be a drinking fountain. You need water, now! There it is, but you cannot walk to it; you slide past, a long way past, to a room where a boy is sitting in front of a monitor, typing on a keyboard. He stops occasionally to drink from a mug on his desk, but you cannot reach it. You can read what he types:

The Rented House

The college housing agent drove my dad and me on a whole bunch of streets that circled into one another until he got to the house we had rented on Bluebell Drive in Austin. My mom and sister can both drive, but my dad and I can't, so we flew to Texas and they came with the car. The agent talked a lot, and my dad mostly said *mmmmm* or *indeed*, except when he asked about the owners of the house. Dad put his question, as he does, super-indirect, so as not to appear nosy, saying he supposed they had gone to some other college in some other town for a year. Then the man whispered, and so of course I paid attention. No. The owners hadn't gone away like that, more that they were unable to afford their mortgage payments on the house, so they were moving to a cheaper place. I could tell my dad didn't like that news much. It seemed like forcing people out, but Dad only said *mmmmm* again. And then we turned into the driveway of the place. It wasn't anything special, a sort of fake Japanese, with a little courtyard behind the garage and an even smaller one next to the front door.

The housing guy gave Dad the keys, waited while Dad opened the front door, asked if he should show us around, but my dad said no thanks. Dad said the sheet of instructions would be fine and we had already troubled him enough. The agent shook our hands and got back into his car and drove away. Dad and I carried our bags into the house. It smelled a little closed and stale, but I had expected that. So far we had been on this sort of academic deal three times, twice for my dad, and now this would make it twice for my mom. Her appointment had brought us here for a year. Dad would use the time, a year off from teaching for him, to write. Mom would teach a seminar, give some lectures, do some research. The college rented the house for us, a place with two studies, so my parents could just work all the time.

"Whew." Dad was ahead of me, so he blocked my view of the inside of the house. "Uh oh. Your mother is going to have a fit." I looked. Yup.

And I could not blame her. We learned from one previous deal, where we had arrived to find a house full of the owner's personal possessions, closets so full of their clothes that we had not a centimeter for ours, drawers chock-full of junk, that sort of thing. After that deal, my mom had insisted it be in any contract: The owner's stuff had to be out of the house before we came in.

"Guess nobody read the contract," I said.

"Guess not. Well. Let's at lcast see if we can start to cart some of this out before Ginny and Mom get here. Gosh. There are four times as many chairs as we'll need." Each of us picked up a straight-back wooden chair. I followed Dad to the garage, he muttering he hoped it was not already full.

I nearly fell more than once. The place was incredibly crowded. Every bookshelf had rows and rows of framed photographs of kids, dogs, people of all ages, lined up in front of the books. Every inch of wall was hung with more photographs. There they were, faces, people you did not know, all of them looking at you from *their* spot, their home.

The garage was nearly empty when we began. We hauled out five extra dining room chairs and three armchairs from the living room, which still left a couch, three chairs, two ottomans, a coffee table, and two lamps. The room was full.

Next we checked the drawers and closets. Mostly they were empty, but with plenty of dust and creepy little leavings to let us know that no one had cleaned. Fortunately, I found a couple of bottles of spray cleaner and some paper towels, so Dad and I set to work cleaning the drawers and shelves in the bedrooms.

It was your standard American Family layout. There was a girl room and a boy room. But why had this boy and girl moved away and left everything in place? I mean, if their toys were important, why would they leave them all behind? The girl had four shelves of "cute" dolls. When I saw them, I chuckled, thinking how *not* charmed my sister would be. Ginny had never been a doll person. The beds were left made up, but Mom would be bringing our own stuff.

I passed on to where Dad was groaning, "Look at all this. A football card collection. . . . Tomorrow we'll get boxes and put away their rogues' gallery, collections, whatever books we can. What is this, a museum?"

Dad and I worked and worked, opening windows, cleaning closets and drawers, vacuuming. That house had a stickiness about it, so you didn't want to touch anything. We washed the kitchen shelves, and all the dishes and all the utensils in the kitchen. We lost track of time, forgot dinner, and, at some point, fell asleep in the living room.

I heard the bell; with my eyes still closed, I dragged myself to the front door. Dad was there just ahead of me, opening the door. Mom, instead of coming inside, reeled backwards as if she had been struck. Dad ran out to her, hugged her, fussed over her.

"Trip bad? You are pale."

"No. Sorry. It's this . . ." She looked past Dad, over his shoulder, but not at me, beyond me into the house. Just then, Ginny, who had been pounding on a back window, came around the side of the house, asking me if I had slept in my clothes, suggesting that Dad and I had had *some* party, and so on.

After a good long look, Mom did come inside, but with a shiver. While she went through the place almost at a run, clearly not liking what she saw, I was thinking, Hah. She should have caught it before we got to work. When I said so, Mom gave me a wan smile, said we should give our faces a quick wash and go out for breakfast, said we needed good food before we could deal with that place.

At the time, I thought my mom was overreacting a bit. That's what I thought.

While Dad and I got cleaned up, Ginny and Mom brought in some of our stuff from the car and put it in the lightest, most neutral room in the house, one we had cleaned thoroughly during our work session the previous night. That was the second study, and had been the easiest to clean because the owners had used it as a small, and I mean small, apartment rented out to a graduate student. It had a desk and a lamp and a couch-bed, and a bathroom just about big enough for a toothbrush. It was the only room in the house not full of books and photographs and knickknacks. Ginny brought in Grace, and he and I smooched a bit and talked. Grace, you have to understand, was a blue and white parakeet, a thoroughly mellow, stress-free, very smart bird. He was named Grace because when we got him he was a young bird, and we were told he was a female. When he got older, his markings showed us that Grace was a male, but he already knew his name, so we decided that Grace was short for Your Grace, a proper title for a noble bird.

Mom and Ginny and Grace had spent the night in a motel. They'd gotten up early, phoned us, but got no answer. They decided the phone must not be working, so they drove over, hoping they could make it in time to have breakfast with us. We checked the phone. It worked. Dad shrugged. "We were beat, slept through it."

We went for breakfast, then stopped on the way home for groceries, and for boxes to pack away the owners' stuff. When we got back to the house, Mom set to work like a dynamo, giving the rest of us orders all the while. Ginny first packed up the girl room, then drove to the supermarket for more boxes.

My first job was to take the food from the kitchen to the garage. Dad said but what about cockroaches, aren't they a problem in this part of the country? That's when I got the brilliant idea to put all the food they had left into the empty freezer that stood in the garage. I filled it with all the half boxes of cereal, the coffee, the sugar and spices from the cupboards.

Doing that job was the best part of the day. Once Ginny got back with more boxes, I had to do the boy room. Mom set to work on the photographs in the living room, hall, and master bedroom. Dad started packing the large study, which was almost as crammed with stuff as the living room. Even the desk had rows of pictures, all staring right at you. "Do you suppose," Dad asked nobody in particular, "these people assumed that leaving so much of themselves behind would make the place more friendly to others?"

Mom muttered about the contract.

I looked out at the bright Texas sunshine, but did not expect to feel much of it that day. To ease my pain at being indoors, I put on my headphones, loaded my player with a tape of my favorite sounds, and set to work.

It wasn't much fun. The books of baseball cards, football cards, and stuff all stuck to my hands, the way plastic wrap clings to you when you try to take it off a package. It made me tired. Then I stripped the bed, including the mattress cover, which was kinda gross with bloodstains. I assumed that the kid must have had nosebleeds, and folded the stuff up and put it into a box. I was carrying boxes out to the garage, thinking I'd ask mom if she had brought mattress covers, when Ginny cried out, then began to sob.

Now, my big sister is not the crying type. She had given up her last summer at home to drive out to Texas with us, to help out and be with us instead of working back home and being with her friends before they all went to college. She is tough and does what she decides to do, but right then she sounded pretty close to hysterical. I dropped the boxes and ran to her. Ginny had Grace in her hand. She was crying and stroking him, and he was dead in her hand.

Ginny and I were crying. First our parents tried to comfort us, saying maybe the trip had been too much, but they knew he had traveled with us many times. Ginny said it straight out, that it was this creepy house that killed Grace, and then my parents stopped trying to comfort us.

"Well," said my mom. "I sure don't like the mood of the place." She took out the contract and read over it, then threw up her hands and said, "Douglas," in that voice that means my dad forgot something important. He read it, and then Ginny read it and I read it, and where it should have said the people had to have all their possessions out of the house and the house clean, it did not say anything. The space was blank. My dad looked bewildered, then phoned the housing agent, who said we could not get out of the contract, said there was no other house for us in the "current tight situation." Period. We were stuck in the place. My dad took the blame for having neglected to check the contract before he signed it. But, even though I did not say anything, I was sure I had seen Dad initial exactly that section. I was sure I had read it over his shoulder. But, with Grace dead, and the oppression of that house, I was not able to hold on to being sure. I did not believe myself, and so I did not say anything that day. And so we mourned for Grace and we cleared out as much as we could of those people, and we told ourselves that Grace had *not* died because we had brought him into that house. We said he must have been sick. I wrapped him in a handkerchief and put him into a small box, and I buried him in the back garden of that house on Bluebell Drive.

The rest of the summer passed. We spent as much time as we could outside of the house. We explored Austin, each and every campus of each and every college. We explored the lakes, the Colorado River, the Capitol, the parks and libraries. Back at our rented house, we never shut ourselves in. As often as possible, we ate out on the patio. With all the photographs gone, the place was less creepy, but still it was odd. Nearly every morning, while making my bed, I'd discover a hair on the pillow. It was not one of mine, not from any one of our family. I knew our colors. Once I found a long and brownish-blond one, another time it was red, another gray. I hated finding those hairs so much that I carried each and every one clear out of the house and straight to the trash can, but I never mentioned them.

In September, just before Ginny went away to college, one more thing happened. It was Dad's day to cook. I was looking forward to the meal, the good food, and to after dinner, when Dad would take out his fiddle and play. It would be one of those good/sad evenings, the sort you have before something in your life changes, before your big sister leaves. I'd watched Dad put up beans to soak, chop stuff for hours, and cook, fiddling with his special blend of seasonings, adding them with flourish. I had been hanging around the kitchen, trying to sneak a taste, which Dad never allows. He sniffs his creation to decide what herbs and spices they need. He claims the nose is the tool of a great chef, and that tasting only spoils the appetite and the dish. I got no taste.

Dinnertime came. I was faint with hunger. The table looked great, heaped with stacks of tortillas and all the trimmings. Finally Dad dipped his ladle in the pot and brought up . . . that thing. It was a long thick braid of human hair. Mom gagged. Even soaked with chili you could see it had been blondish-brown, a kid's hair. Heck. We'd seen enough photographs in that house to recognize the kid with blondish-brown braids. It was so gross that Dad carried the whole thing straight out to the trash, pot and all.

Our appetites destroyed, we had a whole lot of time to ask ourselves who had been able to get in and put it there, and why.

There was one good thing: After that night, the hairs never again appeared on my pillow.

Ginny went to college. Mom and Dad went to work. I started school, but never found anyone to hang out with; besides, that house had me thinking about it nearly all the time. I spent most of the rest of that year in libraries around Austin. At first, I didn't know how to start looking. I mean, I wanted to know about oppressive houses. But then I thought of the individual things, the hairs on my pillow, the blood on the mattress cover. I needed more information. I interviewed my family, though they never knew that's what my questions were. What did I learn? Well, first of all, it wasn't just *my* mattress cover; every mattress cover in that house was stained with blood. You could say the people were bleeders and slobs. Or, you could say something else.

Now, my mom, she's a professor of anthropology, and it was in some of her books that I got my first clues, even though my mom does not believe at all in ghosts or vampires or anything connected with witchcraft. I asked her why she had staggered backwards that first morning when Dad opened the door. She thought back, and then got all pale, but quickly recovered herself, saying that Dad had looked pretty bad. I asked, bad how? and she said unshaven, rumpled, unlike himself. She then added that she had felt our tension. I asked if she had felt evil in the house, and she laughed.

Well, I looked in lots of books in every library in town. I did research. I took notes. I found out that blood and hair and photographs, and, well, any parts of certain inhabitants of a place can be left to take over intended victims. I found out that some beings can exist forever if they can be replenished from the living. I found out that eating one bite of food corrupted by such beings will give them power over their intended victims. I learned lots, if you believe in it, and I did. I was convinced that the rented house had been witched, and I thought that by putting their possessions, blood, and corrupted food away from ourselves, we had escaped them.

The academic year ended. We went home, but before we did, I dug up the box from the backyard, the box in which I had buried poor Grace. I took him home, to bury in our backyard, corny as that might sound to some people.

We went home, but now have been brought back, and accused. The neighbors say the owners never came back to the house. They say we must have done away with them. We were peculiar, they claim, keeping to ourselves the way we did. One neighbor said he saw us put a pot in the trash. The garbage man, when he was questioned, said he remembered it well because it was a perfectly good pot, so he lifted the lid and looked inside. He saw the chili and the braid and thought what strange people we must be. Now the pot and the braid are seen as evidence against us. The police have looked at all the things stored in the garage. They say who but murderers would pack away things like that? They say the bloodstains on all the mattress covers prove we are murderers. They say there are fingernails, hair, blood, and skin in the half boxes of cereals, in the flour and sugar in the freezer, and they ask us, "Why?" All these people are calling my mother "that woman, a professor of ritual cannibalism!" They are accusing us of witchcraft, of cannibalism, and even my reburying of poor dead Grace is used against us. We are accused, and all we did was stop those creatures from taking our lives to feed theirs.

You find yourself sitting on a bench in The Gallery Pitu, no longer sticky and sweaty, but nevertheless uncomfortable. No. You do not like the idea of the undead sprinkling themselves into your food as they tried to do to that boy's family. You shake yourself, trying to gather up energy to look some more or to go home. On the floor next to the bench are a guitar case and a beat-up duffel bag. At the end of the gallery, the blond young man you saw in the park yesterday is standing near a huge, slowly spinning globe. He looks over at you.

"Hello."

"Hi."

He holds an oblong black plastic box, which he points at the globe.

"Look at this." He beckons for you to join him.

"What is it?"

"You point it at the globe and press the button. If the artist has been to the place you choose to strike with the beam, you go there, and . . ." He stops talking, frowns as he searches the face of the globe.

"I thought you were going home today?" you ask.

"Yes, but . . . before . . . I thought of seeing something first."

"What if the artist has not been to the place you strike with the beam?" you ask.

"Then you are the one to go there, to see what you see," he explains. "I was thinking of Alma Ata. See it there, the capital of Kazakh."

"It's far."

"Then there's Berkeley, USA." He nudges you.

"That's far, too."

"Where shall it be? Want to go together?"

Before you can answer, an intense blue light flashes from the black plastic controller, and the gallery is gone.

You are alone, walking up a street, about a block behind a boy who is looking back over his shoulder, a boy not at ease.

You turn to see what can be back there, listening all the while to a voice telling you: This is one you know.

Henry and Vilma

Every girl in the seventh-grade class of Dr. Martin Luther King, Jr., Middle School in Berkeley, California, agreed that Henry was a good-looking guy. One of the teachers had even called him "Handsome Harry." Actually, Henry was the sort of kid everybody likes, good at sports, good in his studies, soft-spoken, friendly, funny. Henry had the sort of thick dark eyelashes girls would kill to have themselves, and a grin to melt your heart. He was a good kid, but he did do something, more than once, that his mama didn't know he did.

You see, Henry lived on a street that was a little bit steep, a typical Berkeley street, on a block of one-story houses, each with a small garden in front. One of those houses belonged to an old woman. That old lady had straggly white hair, a pasty white face with many folds of skin hanging down. Her eyelashes and eyebrows were white, the rims of her eyes pink. And, she said things. Her name — Henry wasn't sure if it was a first name or a last name — was Vilma. When she said something, Henry could never be sure he understood her. Henry was just a little bit scared of her.

The thing that Henry's mama did not know about was that Henry had — more than once — dashed up the walk of Vilma's house, rung her doorbell, and run away. He was *sure* old Vilma had never seen him, never guessed who played the trick.

In the winter of the year Henry was in the seventh grade, in the middle of one chilly, moonless night, it happened that Henry heard a *scratch, scratch, scratching* at his window. He jumped out of bed, raised the shade, lifted the latch, and pulled open the window to see what made the noise.

There, right outside his bedroom window, stood Vilma. The nails of her fingers were painted blood red. Her mouth, too, was red; red as blood. Leaning toward Henry, Vilma demanded, "Do you *know* vat I do vit my long rrrred nails, and my rred, rruby lips?"

Henry, this time, understood every single word Vilma said. Terrified, he slammed the window shut, snapped the latch, and yanked down the shade. He dove under his covers, where he trembled all the rest of the night.

The next morning his mama and his daddy did not mention any noises in the night, and Henry kept quiet about his visit from Vilma. He was not only scared of Vilma, but scared she'd tell his parents about the tricks he had played. Henry took the long way to school that morning, so he didn't need to pass Vilma's house.

Once he got to school and saw his friends, he forgot about Vilma and had a pretty good day. At dinnertime, he ate like a horse. Henry did yawn once or twice over his homework, which made his dad raise his eyebrows when he looked at Henry over the top of his book, but Henry's dad didn't say anything, so Henry went to bed at the usual time, and fell right to sleep.

In the middle of the night, Henry heard at his window a *scratch, scratch, scratching*, and a *tap, tap, tapping*. Henry ran to the window, planning to tell that old Vilma to go away. But when he opened the window, he saw her blood red nails, and her blood red lips, and Henry could not say a word.

"*Do you know* vat I do vit my long rred nails and my rrred rrruby lips??!!!!"

"No," hissed Henry, shutting the window, the shade, and even the curtains. The rest of the night Henry shivered under the covers, but did not hear another sound at his window.

The next morning at breakfast, Henry slumped, dragging his spoon through his cereal, hardly eating. His mama stopped packing her book bag long enough to feel his forehead.

"I'm not sick." Henry shrugged.

"Looks like you need more sleep, my man," Henry's daddy suggested.

"I'm fine." Henry tried to look lively.

Henry did his best to appear full of life that night after dinner, too. He talked for a long time with his daddy about the class field trip to a tide pool. Henry looked long and hard at every book for little kids his mama had brought home to review for the library journal. Henry tried every way to Sunday to stay up as long as he could, but when his parents said *bedtime*, Henry had to go.

Scared as he was, Henry was more tired. He fell asleep immediately, and slept a sleep that was deep, deep, deep.

In the middle of the night there was a *scratch*, *scratch*, *scratching*, a *tap*, *tap*, *tapping*, and a *rap*, *rap*, *rapping* at Henry's window. Henry hid from the sound, but it just got louder. Henry's parents might hear. Then Vilma might tell about how Henry had been ringing her doorbell and running away. Henry had to get up out of his bed. Henry opened the curtains, raised the shade, turned the latch, lifted his window.

Vilma leaned clear into the window, right up close to Henry's face. *"Do you know vat I do vit my long rrred nails and my rrred rrruby lips?"* Vilma waved her fingers right in front of Henry's eyes.

"Wwwwhhat?"

Her eyes glittering, Vilma placed one finger, with its long, blood red nail, right on her red ruby lips and said, "BRRRRRRRRRRRRRRRRR-RRRRRR!!!!!!!!!!!!"

At Vilma's finger and lip babble, Henry jumps just about out of his skin, and so do you; except that you are startled right out of that time and place. You land back in the gallery. The blond, bearded young man from the Faeroe Islands is gone, but his guitar and duffel bag remain where they were, next to the bench. Through the plate-glass window you can see the park, which is full of people. The sky has cleared. The sunshine is bright on the lilacs, pale bluish-purple ones and white ones, blooming along one side of the fence. You are thirsty, and a bit edgy. Where is that drinking fountain? You do not see it in the spot where it was not so long ago. Should you go to the park, drink water, stretch your legs a bit? Should you go for a run, use up some of the energy you have accumulated as you have been sent from place to place here in the gallery? But, if you leave, who knows if the show will be here *when you return? The artist is said to be willful. You could come back and find the walls bare, the door locked. Maybe you can find the fountain. You walk. Over there, in the corner, is a bicycle with two full water bottles. What the heck. You can ride it where it takes you, pedal while you drink from the bottles, and see what then.*

Radio Bimbos

Don't even think that I'm good looking. No great bod, no great face. Yeah, I'm mellow, like myself just fine, but I have no illusions. I am definitely not hot. Got that?

My voice is, well, acceptable. That's how I got the job.

I guess.

It was after school. The station is about ten minutes out of town by bicycle. I went with my bud, Leo, who had been the DJ for an after-school radio program. Leo was leaving for college, not the one here in town, but like really away, to another state. He said I'd be crazy not to take his DJ job. I wasn't sure. I liked Leo, but his program had been a dud. I'd never met anyone who listened to it, never heard of anyone who listened to it. Leo always claimed things were great, but that was Leo's style. Up. Definitely up. It's not my style, but I figured I'd go with

Leo so as not to hurt his feelings. I would not be offered the job, and then I could go home and look for something to eat.

That's how I became Barton Flywheel, DJ.

The station manager gave me a stack of folders of instructions. He said commercials had to be slipped in just so, precise. He said stuff about demographics, and market share, and bulges and peaks and heightened awareness, and "getting the bimbos to tune in." I never did read the instructions, but I got his drift. There was a potential audience out there, listeners, mostly girls in the fifth, sixth, seventh, and eighth grades. They were alone, with nothing to do, outside of town, way out in subdivisions in the suburbs. Those girls bought shampoo, gum, nail polish, and pizza, and records, tapes, CDs. Some of them bought diet stuff.

I didn't follow the station manager's instructions because I could not believe I had the job, and especially not that I would keep it. Why? Well, my voice might have been okay, but my brain? Sometimes I just can't talk. Not that I stutter. I'm silent. It's always been that way, and people who know me know it. In class, if I can't speak, the teachers just go to someone else, let me be until I can click in again. Writing on the board, writing papers, no problem, so people just let me be.

Not on radio. Radio means sound, noise. If

there's silence from a radio, people kick the thing to pieces, throw it out the window. Silence from a radio means *broken*. I knew there could never be silence during my radio broadcast. So, after the station manager had given me the job, I kinda changed the format of the show. If I could talk, and had thought of something to say, I'd talk. Otherwise, I sometimes played a song three, four times, or played more of an album than I'd said I would.

At home I made up some tapes to fill in the silence, had them on a small portable player, so if I had a live mike at my face, and silence in my brain, I could play a bit of tape into my mike, and keep the dreaded silence away.

Making those tapes was wild. See, my Aunt Gertrude is sort of the town character. She teaches a prenatal dance and music class, using Nepalese temple bells, reggae, Mozart, tribal chants, and drumming from all over. She also uses Vivaldi, blues, Turkish belly dancing music, flutes played by shepherds in the mountains of Peru, every kind of music you can think of. I made my own mix from Aunt Gertrude's stuff. Loved it.

Commercials. Yes. I got it when the manager said they were important, so I did not omit them, but clustered them when I could speak. (Just in case I faced a real emergency, I had a second handheld tape player containing taped commercials. I hoped I'd never have to use it.) To make things less boring, I read the live commercials in an order I created that made them talk back and forth to each other. You know, a little drama with the fast food chicken talking to the roach spray, stuff like that. I figured, what the heck. If the program had no listeners, which I was sure was the case, then there would be no complaints. And, if somebody did complain, I'd be fired. Big deal.

Three hours of radio DJ time is a long time. I worked while the music played, did my physics, math, all my homework. I made little games. How fast could I derive the function of that polynomial? Not enough time? Play that song again.

Well, man. I worked for a whole week and did not get fired. The station got a few letters. No. I said no to the suggestion of people phoning in. How can a guy who never knows if he can make a sound talk to people who phone in? I never talk on the phone.

I answered the letters, though. On the air. When I'd get my talking jag, I'd talk, kinda go off on whatever the letter had said. At first they wrote about the music. Yeah, I forgot to mention. Most programs have a format, play only soft rock, or hard, or elevator music, or whatever. Me, I like more than one kind of music, so I played all kinds, back to back, and when you figured that nearly every day there was some of Aunt Gertrude's prenatal dance and sound to cover my speechless spots, it was pretty wide-ranging stuff I was playing on that after-school show.

Then more letters came, and more and more.

"They're listening! The bimbos are listening!" the station manager chortled, clapping me on the shoulder.

"Are they buying?" That was the salesman, grabbing a handful of envelopes from the mail-bag. "Ask them if they're buying."

"Don't care!" the manager snarled. "Radio station's job is to get listeners. It's the job of the commercials to get buyers."

The salesman fumed about market surveys, but left me alone. The businesses that had commercial spots kept on buying them, without any complaints, so I kept on doing what I had been doing. Frankly, I think the sponsors never listened to the show. As the station manager had said when he hired me, the listeners were mostly girls in middle school, the ones who lived way out in all the huge subdivisions that had replaced the wheat. Now, small-town life may be quiet, and farms may not have nightclubs, but both places have things a kid can do. From the letters I got, I concluded that plants in greenhouses have more life than those poor kids out in the 'burbs. Mostly they endured. They had a long bus ride to school, school itself, the ride home, then lots of time alone; TV, radio, whatever, like sleepwalkers, waiting to awake as grown-ups, to what? To fun?

The letters made me sad, partly because I think that having fun takes practice, like riding a bicycle or drawing.

For a couple of months, my handheld tape player and my occasional talking jags, and my random music, went along okay. My show even got a name, Random Radio, a name the kids suggested. The manager still called them bimbos. I never did.

I failed on a clear, sunny, chilly day. I was more than halfway through the show. I'll admit, I was due for a fall. I had really begun to love the success, the glee on the manager's face when he said my show had the most listeners of anything the station did, even the news. I'd even begun to get a little tense, thinking how could I keep on being successful. To calm myself, I'd taken to reading some self-help stuff. I was reading, record near finished: some bubble gum music I had played just for the contrast. The song ended; I put down my book. Time for a bit of talk. I opened my mouth. Uh oh. Silence. No problem. I punched my handheld recorder to PLAY, right there next to the mike, no idea where it was on the tape, what sort of stuff we'd hear. Silence.

The dratted thing was broken. No sound from

the bubble gum record. That mike was off. My hand mike was alive. Me, I choked at the dreaded silence. I punched the other recorder, the one with taped commercials. Silence.

Just listen some time; listen to 2,3,20 seconds of silence. It is forever. That day the silence lasted 35 seconds, maybe 40. My eyes were clenched shut for part of it. Then, as if I'd never clutched in my life, I was able to say, "That, children, was silence. You could hear it any time."

In a sweaty funk, I continued the show. My voice worked, plugged along. I even managed to read aloud some of my self-help book, *Half-Baked Zen*: "Every task, even making a sandwich or folding a towel, should be done with respect for that task, so that work and life are truly known to be worthwhile."

I hit the taped musical commercials. They worked while I read that half-baked sentence again. My Nebraska grandmother said it another way, like what's worth doing is worth doing well. The Kansas grandmother, here in town, says it another way, that life without beauty isn't worth living, so look for the beauty. See it. I was thinking that for those kids living in boxes on what used to be prairie, the beauty might be pretty hard to find amid the boredom. I felt bad for them. I was sure I'd be fired, and I was gonna miss them. Honest, I wasn't thinking I'd miss their corny declarations of love. Naw. I knew I'd miss trying to make them laugh. Thinking along those lines, I nearly missed the end of the taped commercials. Heck. I thought. It didn't matter. Barton Flywheel, DJ, was history.

The show ended. I went slinking out of the station, certain I had blown everything. I'd be fired for sure, which would serve me right for getting so caught up in my "success." I was being all furtive, sneaking around and out to avoid meeting anybody, figuring they did not need to fire me face-to-face. But, nobody noticed. People just kept on doing what they were doing, all four of them. It wasn't a very big station.

I went home.

In the next batch of letters it was "oh wow silence," "how really random," which caused me to change the name of the show once again. I could not believe how lucky I was. I was not fired and nobody threw any radios out of windows and so even the silence stopped being a problem. It was weird though, feeling that whatever I did they loved, all those kids out there. And now it was boys *and* girls listening. I could tell by the letters, though girls wrote more often. I kept on doing the show, watching myself. Sometimes I'd try too hard, the striver bit, going for outlandish, announcing that one-two we'd all fall on the floor now to do exercises to some skate rock while reciting knock-knock jokes as fast as we could. Then I'd feel ashamed and ease up, be mellow, play my little homework games and play the music and think while the music did the work. I did not even worry about possible silence.

Then Huey said what he said at the end of math class. Each of us had had to put one problem and solution on the board. At the end of class, as we were leaving, the teacher said to Huey something about a good job, 'cause the problem he had done was the thorny one of the set. Huey said he'd only been able to do it because I'd helped him on my radio show.

At the time what Huey said barely registered. If I thought anything, it was that old Huey was deflecting a compliment because he didn't want to talk about that problem or any other with the teacher, but only wanted to escape the classroom. Yeah, I had worked that problem while playing some Smetana, actually quite a lot of Smetana because the problem was so tough.

When I got to the station that afternoon, the manager punched me cheerfully on the shoulder, asking me how I liked fame.

Huh?

Talking around his soggy cigar, the manager told me. Old Johnathan on the graveyard, 3–6 AM spot got suddenly, violently sick last night. They had no one to replace him, so somebody had put on a tape of my afternoon show to fill his air time. They got lots of telephone calls. Well, it was 3–6 AM, and the lone engineer couldn't take the calls, so they had no idea exactly how many there had been after the answering machine filled up. The response to me was, he assured me, great, ha-ha. He supposed I'd want a raise.

Then, a few days later someone else mentioned some homework I had been doing during my afternoon show, which had been replayed to cover some bald spot in the manager's programming day. I did think then that maybe I was muttering while doing the homework, or maybe even that the concentration you need for math or physics is strong enough to send out. Maybe I thought that, at first.

Then things went very fast. A package came for me, with a key chain in it, and a note from a girl in the fifth grade: "Hey Barton! Too bad you broke your University of Hawaii key chain. Here's a replacement my brother sent me." My hands started to shake so I could hardly read the words. I had never said anything about that key chain, only thought about it in the instant when it broke, wondered for one second if I could fix it. Then I wondered if I'd ever go to Hawaii. The whole thing took a minute, too trivial to mention even on really random radio.

More and more letters came, chatty letters. It was exhausting reading them, hoping they were regular letters, but feeling sweaty and creepy when one or another would reply to things I knew I had not said aloud over the air.

It got worse. Turn on the radio to that station and you could find me in dribs and drabs twenty-four hours a day. Yeah. The manager was using five- and ten-minute bits, or whole shows on tape when he needed to fill space. It was random and frequent, which meant more and more people heard me, more and more listeners began to talk and write back to things I'd been thinking while I was on the air. I never knew when someone would say, "Oh yeah. I agree with you about raisins in oatmeal," or "Thanks for the help with that problem set," or "I think you're nuts! Who cares if they changed the stupid ending of a stupid book to make a stupid movie!"

I tried not thinking while the music or commercials played. What a joke. It was like when somebody says, Don't think of water. Of course you do. Well, I tried to keep far from the mike while music played. That did not work. I tried, hard, to keep my thoughts to myself, and man-oh-man; not only could I not stop my mind from running off, but I thought about things I never ever wanted to say, and especially not to send out over the air.

The day after I tried my do-not-think bit, a girl I hardly knew walked up to me as I was going into my physics lab. "What kind of pervert are you?" She was spitting mad. "Keep your sleazy remarks to yourself or I'll tell my mother to have that crummy station shut down!"

I knew I had no choice. I had to quit.

The station manager shouted, Did I think I was such hot stuff that I could leave him to go national, 'cause if I did I should know that they owned me, owned my taped shows to play forever if they wanted. They owned the name of the show. They owned it, Bimbo!

Like I said, I have no illusions. Except, I like to think that what's in my head stays there unless I say it out loud. If I had a choice, I'd prefer my old problem. I mean, I thought I had lived pretty well with those bouts of silence that came on me. But hey. I'm mellow, spend my afternoons taking long bicycle rides through the countryside — now that I'm unemployed.

Barton Flywheel, former DJ, pedals faster and faster, leaving you panting, hot and thirsty, sticky all over, and falling farther and farther behind as you pedal more and more slowly. With a sigh of relief, you watch your bicycle float away. You, meanwhile, close your weary eyes, fall backwards onto something soft, firm. You open your eyes to find yourself in a huge room, perhaps a warehouse, sitting on a pile of oriental rugs. More rugs are stacked to the right and left, filling every inch of space on the floor. Other rugs hang on the walls. Each stack contains rugs of a single color, with the shades running from dark, on the bottom, up to light. You look down. The ones on which you sit are of the shades of sand, from gray to peach.

There are people everywhere in the room, sitting on piles of rugs, standing in doorways, talking, smoking water pipes, drinking tea, drinking coffee. Others move among them with trays. Someone offers you a towel and a bowl filled with water on which float the petals of pale pink roses. Gratefully, you wash your hands and face. While you are thus occupied, an old woman brings tea, offering it first to a girl who sits on your right. Peering out of the folds of the towel with which you continue to dry your face, you study that girl.

She is one of those people born beautiful, to remain beautiful every minute of her life. Such a one easily arouses jealousy in observers, casual or otherwise, but this girl's eyes are thoughtful. She wears western clothes; the others in the room are in the robes or loose trousers of the Middle East. The guy from the Faeroe Islands pokes his head in the doorway, waves, calls out, "I'm off for home. I got to Alma Ata, where I fell in love with a girl who is too young. I'll go home to make a song and wait. Did you find yourself in California?" Not waiting for an answer, he leaves with a last wave good-bye.

The girl returns his wave, says in your language, "Mmmm, I remember him, from The Gallery Pitu."

Before you can reply, the room falls silent, listening. Musicians appear, and a singer. The music begins. A ballad is sung, not in any language you know. You, nevertheless, understand every word.

Damascus

In the city of Damascus, quite near to the street called Straight, the street some say is the oldest bazaar in all the world, there lived two women. All their lives they had known one another, as young girls, then as women, the one a shopkeeper, wife to a shopkeeper, the other a midwife. Now, that midwife had an amazing talent. She could read the future of every baby she delivered. All the neighborhood knew the truth of her predictions. She had foreseen the beauty, as well as the wonderful marriage it would bring, in the red and wrinkled fist of a newborn girl. She had seen the travels and adventures as a sailor, and had foretold the marvels he would tell, in the face of a baby boy who looked at birth too weak to live until sunrise. All this and more had been foretold by the midwife. Some of it had been sad, the sadness told soon to lessen the later pain.

When the woman who was a shopkeeper, wife to a shopkeeper, learned that she would have her own baby son, she was quite naturally excited, and eager to hear what her friend the midwife would foretell upon delivering the baby. The shopkeeper had great hopes, of course, hopes for the future of the child. And, she was quite pleased when her friend the midwife looked into the face of her newborn son and said that his fame would be sung throughout the world.

Ahhhh, the new mother sighed. Now that was wonderful. She watched and waited, looking every day at her little son for the signs of coming greatness.

Alas. He was an ordinary baby, a most ordinary little boy. Once, when someone shouted "Fool!" at him, the woman brightened. Perhaps her son would be a holy fool, chosen by God for something special. But, nothing came of that.

The boy had no remarkable talents. He was ordinary in his studies, ordinary in his work, in his taste in food and music. He was not the strongest porter in the marketplace, nor the swiftest, nor even the slowest, nor the weakest. He married an ordinary young woman.

Ahha. At the marriage, his mother had new hopes! Perhaps her son would be the father of a nation, famed in all the world for his many children. But no. He had a most ordinary number of children. Watching and waiting were not quietly done by the mother. Often, *often* she demanded that her midwife friend repeat the prediction. Often she demanded that her friend reveal when it would come true. Often she cried, "Tell more of the wonders my son will do!"

Always, always, the midwife replied, "Told you then, and tell you now, and tomorrow if that day is permitted to me. The fame of your son will be sung throughout the whole wide world."

After a time, relations between the two women cooled, though who could blame the midwife for the breach?

Years passed, and still more years, until the midwife and the mother were both very old women, and the ordinary son was a stooped and tiny old man, so frail that he could no longer work as a porter in the bazaar. Instead, he carried, shaking and rattling in his two hands, trays of tea to the shopkeepers while they bargained with their customers.

It happens that the bazaar in Damascus, on the street called Straight, the bazaar that may be the oldest in the world, is a place crowded beyond belief. The goods tumble out of the shops: rugs and lamps, spices, glassware, knives, and pendants. On the narrow passage, throngs of people press: shoppers, gawkers, porters, thieves.

One day, as the most ordinary old man sat in a shop drinking his glass of tea, there came down the street called Straight, a porter on a bicycle. On the handlebars was balanced a huge crate of bright and beautiful oranges, oranges piled above the rim of the crate. The porter pedaled slowly toward the place that was his destination.

Among the throng on the street that day was another porter, a strong man bent double under a bale of rugs. That fellow sweated, able neither to see nor to hear because of his burden. Others made way for the crate of oranges balanced on the handlebars of the bicycle. Only one person failed to make way: the rug porter, whose wares snagged the corner of the crate, tipping it so that the oranges tumbled into the street. The pile of rugs, too, was dragged from that porter's shoulders.

At once the bicyclist began to shout. The porter of rugs returned insult for insult. At such times weapons appear; old scores are settled; riots destroy the work of a lifetime; and there is anger left over for next time. The bicyclist moved toward the rug porter, his raised fist clenched.

At once, the old man, that most ordinary son, put down his glass of tea, dashed out of the store and through the crowd with agility that was astonishing. With his two hands, the old man reached up, took the fist of the angry bicyclist, and kissed it.

The two porters dropped their fists, the crowd murmuring approval. Watchers stooped to pick up the oranges, not missing a single one, and returned them to the crate. Four passersby helped the rug porter resettle his burden upon his shoulders. The bazaar resumed its normal pace. Only the nimble thieves and pickpockets were disappointed that there had been no brawl. The old man slipped away to finish his tea.

The story was sung that night by one of those street singers one finds in a bazaar. He called his ballad "The Thieves Disappointment," which made people laugh. A stranger, a visitor to Damascus, heard the song and took it to his homeland, where he sang it in another language. In time, both versions were sung in Damascus, on the radio and in the streets, and, so we are told, in other languages and countries around the world. But even when she heard the song, the poor mother was not satisfied. One last time she scolded her old friend, "Is this song what you promised? You told me his name would be known throughout the wide world."

"Told you. I told you," the midwife replied. "His *fame* would be known throughout the wide world."

When the song ends, the audience, with cheers and applause, demands that it be repeated. The singer and musicians comply, while tea and sweets are passed among the rest of you, the listeners. After the ballad, other favorites are requested and performed. You, tired beyond belief, doze. When you awake, the musicians and singer have gone. The few people who remain are sitting hunched over their account books. That beautiful girl with the thoughtful eyes is still sitting next to you. When she sees that you are awake, she asks if you are ready to go back to The Gallery Pitu. You reply that so far you have never had much say in the matter.

"You need to hang on to something. Here." She takes an orange from her pocket. Stamped in purple on its bright skin is the word DAMASCUS. "Hold on to half of it."

You do, and find that you and she are back

in the gallery, with sun and park and lilacs as they were.

"Should I put the orange back over there, on the one called Damascus?" you ask.

The girl shrugs. "You're allowed to keep a memento."

"See this piece?" she asks, gesturing toward an oddly configured montage of photographs. You must twist your neck this way and that to make out glimpses of a road, fields, a heavily wooded curved drive, an old house with a broad porch across the front, and snapshots of a boy whose age changes, but not the expression on his face. There is also a bookmark, which hangs from a red thread, turning slowly in a draft. On the front is a colored printed bookish joke. On the back is a small drawing in pencil of an old-fashioned automobile. You hear, as you study the photographs, the roar and swish of an automobile passing close by, as if it were in the room. Tired as you are, it startles you, and you flinch.

"What you heard," the girl says, "was the sound of the car. The artist got it just right."

The Phantom Touring Car

For years I heard the arguments: The car was good, a guardian angel car that saved us. No! The car was evil. No again, absolutely no; the car was imagined, pure imagination.

One thing I know, because I saw it. The car had a ghostly beauty. It was a silver car, stately, old-fashioned. Mostly, the kids who saw it stared in admiration. Mostly the parents, driving their own cars, did three things simultaneously: saw it, gasped, slammed on their brakes. Afterwards, they sighed with relief. The car, the one we called the Phantom Touring Car because someone's dad said it was an old and elegant touring car, with a chauffeur and all, that car was only seen in one spot, and only when there was danger.

The danger came about because of what my father called the lay of the land. The pike, Lamston Pike, ran, straight as a pike — the stick, not the fish — from the capital of the country to the university town, Lamston. The land sloped down from the road, sloped down and stayed wet. The pike crossed over the river at one point. After that bridge, the river ran parallel to the road for quite a way. The low, wet land that lay between the river and the road was what people call a flood plain. When it rained, you could be sure that land flooded. Some of the land was, nevertheless, woods, the trees somehow surviving with wet roots. Most of the land was used as a huge sod farm, vast fields of lovely velvety grass, with huge flocks of birds whirling up from feeding, then floating down to feed again. I spent years of my life sitting in classrooms, dreaming out the windows, watching those sod fields, the birds, the mowers, the cutting and rolling of sod, the thick mud, the new green crop. Some days I watched the sky, other days the fog, as it rose silver gray off the river, then danced and waved through the trees, reaching out across the fields, across the pike, right up to the classroom windows. That was the lay of the land that produced those fogs, and the danger for those who traveled the pike.

The school we attended was in the middle of the pike, Lamston Pike School, a private school, founded generations ago by the Lamston family for their special kid, and for all his brothers and sisters and for all the special kids of their friends. Each kid is in that school for some peculiar reason. Some kids are there because they can't work in a regular school, public or private. Some are there because they won't work, anywhere. Some because they are so shy they curl up and die out there in the real world. Me? Well, my daddy chose the place for several reasons, one of them being that he is raising me alone, and has to work long hours. When I was little it mattered that Lamston Pike School had a really good after-school program. You know, baby-sitting.

My classmate, Lamston Lamston Lamston the fourth, had few pleasures in life. One of them was to tell me, especially, what weirdness had sent each of us to that school. He said that daddy first put me in Lamston because he did not want me to be one more black kid with just one parent in some public school, a kid they would assume is dumb and send to all the remedial stuff. Lamston said that at Lamston Pike, daddy paid lots so I could dream or work as it suited me. Lamston, who really was the fourth one to have that name, started at Lamston Pike School, the one his family had founded, the same time I did, first grade.

Most of the other kids, and all of the teachers, had trouble with Lamston, who was your basically dissatisfied, faultfinding, miserable kid. Nothing was worthy, and Lamston made it his exclusive business to tell you so and exactly why. Even I, who regularly argued with him, had to admit that often he was painfully clearsighted, painfully accurate. Consequently, everybody tried to avoid him.

But even Lamston, who sneered at sports, music of any sort, skateboards, friendship, food, you name it, was, from the start, curious about the Phantom Touring Car.

The car, the school, and the pike were definitely connected. When those fogs rose from the river and spread across the fields, as they suddenly and unpredictably did, the Lamston Pike became a dangerous road. Our school drive was only one of many that opened onto the pike, each of them obscured by bushes, shrubs, vines, or a huge old shade tree. There were, as well, country roads that crossed the pike. Cars speeding from the capital, shooting out on a straight road in bright sunshine, could abruptly hit a thick fog — and an oncoming car. It could happen at any driveway, any intersection, and often did.

The government had posted warning signs and lights along the pike, but they weren't much help. Sometimes, especially if you happened to be out on the school playground, you could hear the screech of brakes, and then, above the pounding of your heart, a crash.

In the fog, school-bus drivers and parents poked along our school drive, creeping along, stopping often, the driver's head out the window to listen for oncoming traffic. All were careful, but sometimes not careful enough to avoid those cars and trucks speeding from the capital or, less often, from the town of Lamston.

We'd all have been dead five times over if it had not been for the Phantom Touring Car. How many times had it come out of the fog, passing right through the car in which we trembled, causing someone's mom or dad to brake so that we all rocked in our seats? Seeing the Phantom, the driver of our car or bus had stopped, stopped in time to avoid being hit by an onrushing truck or car that was no phantom.

Most of the parents and kids at our school discussed the car right after it had been seen, but some of the kids went on about it even when the sun was shining. Some kids were terrified by it, some thrilled. Some parents maintained that it was an illusion, some that it was ghosts, some that it was somebody's guardian angel watching over us all.

Lamston, by the third grade, was among the kids obsessed by the car. He had begun, secretly, to make drawings of it. I saw him, and wondered why he kept them hidden, asked myself if it was because it was so important to Lamston to be down on everything, that he did not want there to be a single exception, not even that one.

On back-to-school night, I found out I was wrong. It started out as the usual deal. The kids' work was displayed on all the bulletin boards. There was punch and cookies in the gym. Your desk had to be perfect, with your notebooks and quizzes all in order. Every kid knew not to have anything there you did not want your parents to see. Lamston's drawing pad was full of assignments; drawings of leaves, insects, the usual. That wasn't the problem. Somehow, he had overlooked another piece of art, on a skinny piece of paper, a bookmark. Actually, it was the back of a bookmark. On the back of that bookmark, Lamston had drawn a picture, a pretty good one, of the Phantom Touring Car, and then left it in his arithmetic book.

Now, there were other drawings of the car, in other kids' desks, and even on the display boards, so it was a tremendous surprise when Lamston's father slammed down that arithmetic book. Right then and there Mr. Lamston made a speech. He made it again when all the kids and parents and teachers were in the gym for refreshments. He got pretty red in the face when he said, "Seeing that car is a classic example of mass hysteria. The figment of someone's powerful imagination has created an image onto which the rest of the children, and some parents, have latched. For the mental health of all of you, that car must cease to be a subject for discussion, an object for artists."

When I asked Daddy if Mr. Lamston could really stop kids from drawing the car or talking about the car, Daddy laughed, said he could try.

Well, the speech didn't stop Lamston, or anybody else, from talking or drawing, though the pictures were never again chosen for displays, and nobody, not even Lamston, ever again left one to be found on back-to-school night. By sixth grade we all laughed. You could draw and display a unicorn or anything else you could imagine, but not the car.

During those years, the Phantom Touring Car passed our school more and more often. When I was in first grade, people only saw it in the thick fogs, but over the years the traffic on Lamston Pike grew heavier. We saw the Phantom Touring Car in rain, in mist and sleet, and once in a blizzard that closed the school.

Lamston Pike School ended with the eighth grade. After that the class split up, going off to all kinds of places, boarding schools in other countries, public schools, private schools, high schools for art or dance or science. I was happy that year, knowing it was the last year, looking forward to high school, to leaving what had been something like a long nap. High school would be alive, real, not dreaming. Lamston IV, of course, disagreed. Nevertheless, he, too, was different that year. He had an air of heightened excitement. Oh, he still criticized every piece of clothing, every gesture, every question, answer, book, movie, every dance. Still, he was somehow keen, on the lookout. I knew he was looking for the car. No matter who else saw it, Lamston was always there.

Afterward, he'd be breathless, describing it, words tumbling. Then, abruptly, as high as he had been, he'd crumble, go all silent and sullen. We'd say he was nuts, shrug, and go on with whatever we were doing.

When we discussed the car, as we often did, it was Lamston who provided every detail, every variation on the pattern of its appearance. Even the biggest braggarts in the class quickly learned to beware of ever making any special claims about the car. Make that mistake, and Lamston would grill and argue, growing close to violent, until the teller of tall tales gave up. Lamston never stopped until he was satisfied that he was the one who knew what-when-where-and-how the Phantom Touring Car had performed.

Lamston was there the night Bit got so scared. Five of us were the last ones to leave school that night, the night of our first dance that year, seventh- and eighth-graders from three private schools. Daddy was one of the chaperones, and the rest of us were the clean-up committee, something Lamston never would have done, except that Daddy was giving him a ride home, so he had to. Of course Lamston went to dances. How else could he tell us how utterly worthless they were? So, there we were, Bit and Lamston and Lori and Tink, in Daddy's car, at the end of the school drive, a light rain falling, when up pulls the Phantom Touring Car, going fast. It was approaching straight on, not driving across our path the way it so often happened. Seeing the car, Daddy braked, but then, just as it came into our headlights, it slowed down to a crawl. Of course we looked, stared hard at it. Bit began to whimper, "Oh, it's full of kids, and look how scared and sad they are. Look at their faces pressed against the glass."

Tink shook her head. "Bit, that was the reflection of *our* faces in the windows of the car." Bit covered her eyes. The car disappeared, and Daddy drove on, after waiting to see if some car or truck would speed across our path. The road was empty.

Lamston, for the first time ever, asked a question of a grown-up. He asked Daddy, did he think it was our reflection. Daddy said it was the darndest optical illusion he had ever seen, with our light reflecting off the car, and yet passing through it. Daddy shook his head, said he could not tell for sure if he had seen faces or not.

I had, and was sure Tink had got it right. We had seen our faces, looking as hard as we could, with timid Bit scared to death and seeing her own fear. For days after that Lamston seemed worried. He asked me again and again if I thought there had been other kids. He kept saying that there couldn't, just couldn't, be other kids.

"Other?" I asked him. "Other than whom?"

He didn't answer.

Months rolled by. We saw the car once more, but not so that we could tell if there was anybody inside. Most of the kids were occupied with other interests. Two big events were approaching, graduation and Lamston's birthday, which was the day before graduation. Lamston's parents gave a big party every year on Lamston's birthday. There were pony rides when we were small, hot-air balloon rides when we got bigger. One year the party was on a riverboat. Lamston was never more surly than at these parties. The rest of us went because it was polite, even if he wasn't.

As graduation got closer, I got split up inside, happier, and sadder, feeling a tremendous affection for all those years of dreaming, for the fields of green sod, the flocks of birds, the fog, and for the car. Oh yeah, people do go back for reunions and to visit the old school; but when you are gone, you are gone.

Lamston said he had no such affection. But he had an excitement that increased day by day. Some kids speculated that maybe his parents had finally found some sort of birthday party that would please him. They thought of all sorts of surprises it might be: a trip by jet? or elephants? or something so outrageous even they could not imagine it? Everyone knew that nothing his parents had done had ever pleased Lamston, and somehow I did not think his mood was connected to the party. I wondered if maybe he, too, was glad to be leaving the school, glad to move on to something else. But, when kids talked of schools of one sort or another, Lamston responded with his usual sneer. Lame stuff. When asked where his parents would send him, Lamston said it would be a surprise.

I thought about his mood; expectation is what you'd have called it in anyone else. In anyone else I'd have thought maybe he was looking forward to doing some prank, letting loose mice at graduation, or perhaps firecrackers. No. Lamston would not be gleeful at the prospect of a prank. He was too critical to ever imagine fun. Still, he was strange, made me feel almost ill to be near him. He got taller and thinner, his skin nearly transparent, glowing. His eyes shone. His hands were never still.

The morning of his birthday was a regular school day; the plan for the party was still a mystery to all of us. It was a glorious spring day, with masses of daffodils alongside the road, tulips in the garden in front of the school. I arrived late to school, which I almost never did. As I shut the door of Daddy's car, Lamston was coming out of the school. I waved to Daddy, who drove quickly away. When I turned to go into the school, Lamston called to me softly, "Wait."

I looked, and what I saw made me shake. Lamston's face was transported — no, distorted — with joy. I'd never seen him grin. I could not remember that he had ever smiled.

"Look."

I looked. At the end of the drive, in the bright spring sunshine, the Phantom Touring Car pulled up, stopped. Lamston sighed, his face softened. "Want to come? You're the only one I'd even consider asking." His voice had returned to the normal nasty Lamston tone by the end of the sentence, as he sensed that I would refuse.

"Thanks. No. I like it here."

He shook my hand, formally, with a little bow. His hand was solid, firm, warm. He walked down the drive. The car door swung open. As far as I could tell, the seats were empty. When he reached the car, Lamston turned to me and waved. For once his face looked truly relaxed, mellow, like a real person. I waved back. Lamston got into the Phantom Touring Car and shut the door.

Silently, the car drove away, for the last time.

I did not know then, and still do not know. Was Lamston's dad right? Did someone have an imagination powerful enough to create that car? Was it Lamston? Was he suffering the pain of waiting all those years, trying to get the car to come for him, afraid it never would?

You see it all there in *The Gallery Pitu*, see the boy wave good-bye, see the car drive away, the girl watch it go. You sit very still, after the vision of school and garden have faded. At last the girl turns, faces you.

"Are you the artist?" you ask her.

She shakes her head, "No. This was the only one I knew. How about you?"

"Not the artist; not in the show." Your gesture includes the whole gallery, the park now in shadow.

"You can never be sure." The girl gets up from the bench, walks the length of the room. Without looking back, she grasps the handle of the front door, presses the latch. She opens the door, and steps outside. With one last look back at the gallery, you follow her out the door. The evening air is fresh, cool on your face. Behind you, the door closes; the lights go off in The

Gallery Pitu. And you, outside, you know that whatever you may take away with you, you also leave something behind, something that now belongs to the artist who shows only in The Gallery Pitu.

Author's Note

"My Elder Sister" is my version of a story told by Gary Snyder, a poet and professor at the University of California at Davis, in his book, *The Practice of the Wild* (North Point Press, 850 Talbot Avenue, Berkeley, California 94706). Professor Snyder cites these sources for his version of the story, both by Catherine McClellan: *The Girl Who Married the Bear: A Masterpiece of Indian Oral Tradition* (Publications on Ethnology, no 2, Ottawa, Museum of Man, 1970) and *My Old People Say: An Ethnological Survey of Southern Yukon Territory, Parts 1 and 2* (Ottawa: Museum of Man, 1975).

"Henry and Vilma" is my version of a story I have heard countless times from storytellers in libraries and near camp fires. I believe that Carol Birch has made a recording of it that my youngest child heard and then recounted that same evening, which impressed upon me once again how easily children who are not yet reading learn to tell.

The other stories in this book are ones I have concocted.

About the Author

JUDITH GOROG has a number of creepy tales to her credit. Her newest collection, *Please Do Not Touch*, is a little different from her previous titles — the reader is actually involved in the stories. Sort of.

Ms. Gorog's inspiration for this story collection comes from her best and oldest friend, who wrote about an artist who filmed his entire apartment and sold the film. The viewer was then able to "snoop" around the apartment, very much like a spy — or a fly on the wall!

Ms. Gorog lives in Pennsylvania with her husband, two daughters, and son.